How in the world had his name slipped in? Just to prove how wrong he was for her, Hallie went ahead and listed his pros and cons:

Pro: Good father

"Not enough facts for a firm opinion." She drew a line through it.

Pro: Nice butt

"Oh, for Pete's sake!" That one got two lines through it.

Cons: Moody. Volatile. Heartthrob. Passionate!

Cody Brock didn't belong on her list. Because around him, Hallie felt dizzy and emotional. Passionate.

Dangerous sensations she could never ever allow herself to give in to again.

Dear Reader,

Picture this: You're thirty, single and on a husband hunt! You've done your research, highlighted the eligible bachelors, made lists and spreadsheets, bar graphs and flow charts...and you've narrowed your choices down to a millionaire, a cowboy and the boy next door.

That's exactly what three American Romance heroines have done—and we're about to pick up their stories in the hilarious HOW TO MARRY trilogy. Here, Mindy Neff introduces you to the third bride-in-waiting who has her eye on the boy-next-door type—but surprises are in store with her neighbor Cody Brock.

Find out if these three men can show these three women a thing or two about passion—the most important part of a marriage!

Happy reading!

Debra Matteucci
Senior Editor & Editorial Coordinator
Harlequin Books
300 East 42nd Street
New York, NY 10017

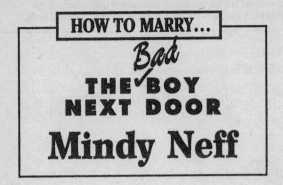

HOW TO MARRY...

THE *Bad* BOY NEXT DOOR

Mindy Neff

Harlequin Books

TORONTO • NEW YORK • LONDON
AMSTERDAM • PARIS • SYDNEY • HAMBURG
STOCKHOLM • ATHENS • TOKYO • MILAN
MADRID • WARSAW • BUDAPEST • AUCKLAND

For my daughters:
Julie, Sharri, Robin and Shannon.
Because you all make me so proud!

ISBN 0-373-16679-6

THE BAD BOY NEXT DOOR

Printed in U.S.A.

Prologue

Hallie Fortune felt a sense of expectancy, a surrealistic, intangible urgency, as if something magical were in the air.

She shook her head. What fanciful nonsense. If there was one thing Hallie wasn't, it was fanciful. Down to earth, levelheaded, practical. That was her. Good, sweet, Hallie Fortune.

Damned near *thirty-year-old* Hallie Fortune.

She groaned and needlessly straightened the photographs on the fireplace mantel. It was probably the phone call from her cousin, Maggie that had her feeling this way.

Destiny, Maggie had said. *Grab it with both hands and run with it.*

A germ of an idea had formed while talking to her cousin. The more Hallie thought about it, the more she liked the idea. A scorecard to rate a man's suitability for her purpose.

The purpose of choosing a husband. The *right* husband. A pro and con sort of thing. If Maggie could

rely on a wish list, why not adopt a similar princi-
ple?

As she waited for Tim Levine to pick her up for
the Labor Day barbecue, Hallie ran her finger over
the oak-framed picture of herself and Maggie and
Clarissa standing in front of a fortune-teller's tent at
the SummerFest. The photo had been taken when they
were twelve. Eighteen years ago today.

The urge to drop everything and make the half-hour
drive to the Bridgeport SummerFest was both powerful and confusing. But she couldn't leave Tim in
the lurch. It wasn't the good-girl thing to do.

She smiled at the image of Maggie holding the
green lizard she'd won at the shooting booth. A
beauty, even at twelve, Maggie was a tomboy at heart.
Lord how she'd bragged about her deadeye aim that
had won the stuffed animal. Now the high-fashion
model had quit her job and was off for a new life in
Texas, back to where her roots were.

Destiny.

Hallie's gaze shifted from her cousin to her childhood best friend. She was worried about Clarissa.
Neither she nor Maggie had heard from her in way
too long. But Clarissa did that sometimes—pulled
back when her emotions were on edge.

"Oh, Clarissa, what happened to your millionaire?
Our childhood dreams? Mine and yours and Maggie's?"

Destiny.

But nothing stayed the same. Like the shifting of
the ocean tides, life too, altered. There came a time

when you had to look life square in the face and take stock.

Clarissa and Maggie had recently turned thirty and Hallie would reach that milestone age in just a few weeks. Time to stop subconsciously relying on fate and take destiny in their hands.

Her thumb smoothed over the glass covering the photograph. Clarissa with flame red hair in her too small dress with the too short hem, Maggie with the impish, double-dog-dare me attitude and expression, and herself, somewhat reserved, feeling free at the carnival, free from the turmoil of her parents' bickering.

She remembered the giggling, the camaraderie. And it had been all Maggie's idea....

"Hey, look at that tent! It's Clarissa's fortune-teller," Maggie had exclaimed. Maggie was the boisterous one, the leader of the threesome. She nudged Hallie. "Your last name's Fortune, Hallie. You should go in."

Hallie rolled her eyes. "You don't really believe in that stuff, do you?"

"Come on, cuz', don't be a chicken. It's like an omen, or something. Don't you think so, Clarissa?"

Clarissa shrugged, her cinnamon eyes hopeful yet reserved. "I didn't bring a lot of money with me."

Hallie's innate compassion rose. She'd always been able to come up with a good excuse to slip her friend lunch money without it seeming like charity. She did something similar now, responding to that spark of hope in Clarissa's eyes.

"It won't cost you a dime. I'm the one with the omen name." She wasn't exactly sure what an omen was, but she didn't want to sound stupid and ask. "Since we're all spending the night at my house tonight, that makes me sort of like the hostess. This'll be my treat for all of us. But I get to go first since I'm the one with the right name."

"Yeah," Maggie said. "And if we don't let her go first, she'll chicken out."

"Will not," Hallie said, shooting her cousin a snappy look. Maggie just grinned and the three girls linked arms, smothering nervous giggles.

They stood inside the cool tent, allowing their eyes to adjust from the bright sun to the shadowy interior. Hallie almost did chicken out. It was the hope in Clarissa's eyes that held her steady.

"Come in, girls. Well, hello again, Clarissa." The woman gave Clarissa a special greeting having known her from the neighborhood. "I am Sabrina and this is Maurice." Maurice, Hallie realized, was a cute little monkey with inquisitive brown eyes who wore a tiny cone on his head and a miniature vest the same bright magenta color as the fortune-teller's elaborate turban. "What can I do for you today?" the gypsy asked.

Hallie sucked in a breath and grabbed at her courage, moving forward to sit at the three-legged stool. "We're here to have our fortunes told. I'm Hallie Fortune, and with the name and all..." Her words trailed off. She'd just told her name. Shouldn't she have kept that a secret? Just to see if the lady was a fake or something? She wished she knew more about this sort of thing.

She cleared her throat. "I'd like to go first, please."

"Ah, such manners. Let me see your hand, Hallie Fortune."

Hallie held out her right palm, embarrassed at the way it trembled. Sabrina's kohl-rimmed eyes seemed to laugh, yet her bright red lips remained serious and pursed. Bracelets clanged like musical wind chimes as she accepted Hallie's palm, running her long, bright nails over the lines crossing the inside of Hallie's hand.

"Passion," Sabrina murmured.

Hallie almost snatched her hand back. That was something she associated with her parents. Not the mushy kind of passion, but the bitter kind. She almost bolted but changed her mind when she glanced at Clarissa and Maggie. She couldn't ruin this for them. Especially for Clarissa.

"I see compassion and nurturing. And the boy next door."

"What?" Hallie's insides jolted as if she'd just rounded a sharp curve on the roller coaster that plunged on the end of Webster Street. Despite herself, she leaned forward, searching her palm as if the future would rise up in living color.

"You're going to marry the boy next door," Sabrina elaborated, her attention focused on Hallie's palm.

Giddy hope soared within Hallie's heart, but her face flamed when Maggie snorted and started to tease.

"There's no way your mom's going to let you marry Cody Brock!"

Just the sound of his name made Hallie's insides quiver. She'd spent many nights secretly fantasizing about her dark and brooding neighbor, wishing she was older, hating all the bouncy cheerleader types who hung out in front of his house, throwing themselves at him. His house was always getting toilet-papered. The girls made so much noise at it, Hallie knew they were hoping to get caught—by Cody.

Though she'd longed to slip out and join the older girls, hoping for a glimpse or a word from the neighborhood bad boy, she'd never built up the nerve. If she did something sneaky like that and got caught, it would cause her parents to fight. And she never wanted to be the cause of that. She made it a point to be extra good, to keep peace in the family.

Hallie ignored her cousin's teasing and Clarissa's soft giggle. She'd barely heard what else Sabrina had said once Maggie had blurted out Cody's name. So what if she had a crush on him. It wasn't unheard of for a bad boy to marry a good girl. The fortune-teller even said so.

Hallie pulled her thoughts back to the present. Sabrina had gone on to predict that Maggie would marry a cowboy and Clarissa a millionaire.

Destiny. Grab it with both hands and run with it.

Hallie placed the picture on the mantel and wiped at the dust. The boy next door was *literally* out of the question. Cody Brock had left town and hadn't been heard from since. It was the *type* she was in search of now.

She heard a strange jingling and glanced at the mantel clock.

It was six p.m.

Tim, she thought. Punctual as always. Tim Levine was safe, a nice guy, most likely the perfect guy for her. And he was always jingling the change in his pocket. An annoying habit, but one she could tolerate.

When she pulled open the front door, though, she frowned.

No one was on the porch. Yet the sight that greeted her made her tremble. Parked at her front curb was an antique-looking wagon painted bright red and orange, with large spoked wheels…hitched to a horse of all things.

Surely she was seeing things. She heard organ music. A new type of ice-cream truck? she wondered.

Drawn outside despite herself, Hallie glanced up and down the street. Strange how none of the neighbors had come out to comment on the weird sight. Especially Hazel Crowley and George Delong. They were the neighborhood busybodies. Nothing got past those two.

But nothing and no one stirred. Not even the breeze. The hair on Hallie's arms stood on end as if the air were filled with static from an electrical storm. Except there wasn't a cloud in the sky.

Everything was still.

Eerily still.

Her feet moving of their own accord, as if drawn

by a powerful magnet, Hallie stepped off the porch, moving past the impatiens and roses, past the bright yellow daisies with their happy faces clustered together. When she reached the back of the wagon, chills raced up and down her spine.

Sabrina awaited her, a monkey perched on her shoulder. The gypsy hadn't aged a bit, even though it had been eighteen years since she'd seen her. Eighteen years to the day. Labor day.

"Sabrina?" Hallie asked, not quite believing her eyes, yet delighted. As a girl, she'd daydreamed about the flamboyant gypsy, pictured herself related to the woman, traveling with her, searching crystal balls and spreading happiness and hope to multitudes of seeking souls. The fantasies of a good girl longing to do something wild and inappropriate.

"How've you been, my sweet?"

"Good."

"And your life as a nurse? Is it all you'd expected?"

How had Sabrina known she was a nurse? "It's, uh, fulfilling."

"But you're lacking passion."

"I'm not looking for passion," Hallie scoffed.

Sabrina tisked. "The peace you yearn for *and* your passion will knock soon. He is on his way, child."

Was the woman talking about Tim? After all, he should have been here by now. The bank manager was perpetually punctual.

"I see your skepticism, Hallie Fortune. But you

mark my words. Passion is at the root of your problem."

It sure was. She'd watched passion ruin her parents. And she'd been burned by it herself—twice. Once in college—a brief lapse of good judgment. Judgment skewed by screaming hormones that had been awakened by a teenage crush, a crush on a boy she'd foolishly pinned her hopes on.

Still, she'd like to discuss Sabrina's prediction of eighteen years ago, to tell her about the interpretation maturity had helped her realize. But the phone was ringing inside her house. It might be Tim, calling to tell her why he was late. Maybe he wanted her to meet him somewhere instead.

"Sabrina, can you stay for just a minute? Let me just answer that phone." She dashed back up the walk and into the house, her voice breathless as she snatched up the telephone. A dial tone greeted her.

"Darn it." Hurrying back out, Hallie nearly slammed into Tim Levine who'd just mounted the porch steps. She peered around him, excited, afraid, confused, wondering how she would explain that she needed just a few minutes more with the gypsy before they could leave.

The street was empty.

Jingle, clink. Jingle, clink. She glanced down and realized that this time it was the change in Tim's pocket creating the sound.

"Where did she go?"

"Who?"

"Sabrina."

"I didn't see anyone." *Jingle, clink. Jingle, clink.* The coins in his pocket tinkled louder.

"But I was just..." Her words trailed off. Tim's car was at the curb.

There was no way in the world he could have missed an old-fashioned gypsy wagon. Or a horse, for goodness sake.

An eerie shiver worked its way up Hallie's spine.

Had she dreamed the encounter with Sabrina? Hallucinated? Conjured up an elaborate, lifelike image from looking at a childhood picture?

Good, Lord, she was losing it. Big time!

Chapter One

Hallie Fortune had already heard the news. Cody Brock, Parkdale's bad boy was back. She shook her head at the lightning speed of a small-town gossip mill—and at the unexpected shiver that worked its way down her spine. She did *not* consider this an omen, good or otherwise.

Never mind that she'd been thinking about him just last week before the Labor Day barbecue.

When she heard the slam of a car door, she gave in and peeked out the lace curtains of the front room window, ignoring the fact that her fisted grip was seriously threatening the ecru threads of the delicate fabric.

Not only was Cody Brock back after fifteen years, she realized, stunned, he had a baby on his hip!

The sight was so incongruous, she blinked. A humid, summer breeze filtered through the open window, carrying the scent of pear trees and the sound of impatient cursing.

The Chevy Blazer parked in the driveway next door was brand spanking new—if the sticker tags in the window were any indication. Trailered behind was a shiny black-and-chrome motorcycle. Okay, Hallie thought, you can't haul a kid on a Harley so you buy a new truck. Makes sense.

Except Cody Brock was the last man in the world she'd expected to see hauling a baby around.

Feeling like a voyeur, her heart pounding for no good reason, she watched as Cody ineptly juggled keys, diaper bag and squirming baby. He lost his grip on the pink, flowered diaper bag when he used his hip to nudge the back door of the Blazer. Next went an empty plastic baby bottle, bouncing as it hit the concrete driveway. Hallie's first instinct was to rush to his rescue, to at least retape that pitiful excuse for a diaper.

Then she reminded herself this wasn't her problem. She was turning over a new leaf. She was on vacation from her nursing job with a definite purpose in mind—to narrow her choice for a nice, *safe* guy to settle down with. After all, she wasn't getting any younger—and at almost thirty, it was about time she find a husband.

Now was not the time to add another needy person to her list. Not that Cody Brock had ever been needy.

Besides, any minute now, she expected to see the mother of that baby pull in behind Cody's truck. The grapevine hadn't said anything about Cody being married. Then again, the grapevine hadn't said anything at all about Cody Brock in the last fifteen years.

Hallie was pleased to note that, with a few more emphatic words, he'd hitched the kid more securely on his hip. The bottle had been retrieved and shoved in the waistband of his jeans. She raised her brow at that. He'd always been fairly resourceful. The diaper bag now hung from his free shoulder.

Shifting a little, her cheek almost pressed against the glass pane of the window, she saw him move to the front door. Apparently he was having trouble with his key. More muttered curses followed, blending with the increased whimpering of the baby.

Once again, Hallie wondered where in the world this child's mother was.

His gaze lifted and Hallie jerked back, her heart tripping like a jackhammer. She felt like a fool spying on him like this. But Cody Brock did that to her. He held a brooding magnetism that drew her despite her best intentions.

Easing back to the window, she nudged the lace a mere fraction. Cody had given up on the front door lock and had now moved around to the side of the house. Thanks to a particularly vicious storm the previous winter, the fence separating their properties was down, making the two yards appear as one huge lot. Since the Brocks' house had sat vacant for so long, Hallie hadn't been in any hurry to replace the fence. She'd probably have to see to that pretty soon.

Suddenly, there was a loud splintering of glass, followed by the startled wail of the baby. Good Lord, Cody Brock was breaking into his parents' house! Figures, she thought. The guy hadn't changed a bit. Which was really too bad in Hallie's opinion. He was a walking fantasy in tight-fitting jeans and a white

T-shirt that revealed every rock-hard muscle. A pity maturity hadn't brought with it any good sense.

Right on cue, the telephone rang. Tearing herself away from the window, Hallie crossed the room and lifted the receiver.

"My land, Hallie. Did that boy just bust out a window?"

"It appears that way, Mrs. Crowley." Hazel Crowley lived across the street. There wasn't a thing in the neighborhood that escaped her notice—other than phantom gypsy wagons. "I guess he couldn't get the key to work."

"Mercy, Gerald and Miranda would turn over in their graves if they saw such a sight."

"No," Hallie said. "They'd have welcomed him with open arms and you know it." The Brocks had doted on Cody, no matter what he'd put them through.

"You're right, dearie. But...oh, horsefeathers! That grouchy old George Delong's coming up my front lawn. He's such a busybody. Probably expects me to know exactly what's going on in the neighborhood—as if I've nothing better to do with my time but gawk at the neighbors. Oh, piddle. There's the bell now. Why does that man insist on leaning on it that way? Does he think I'm deaf?"

Hallie smiled. George Delong was a grouch, but he was an absolute dear. And Hazel Crowley had a major crush on him, even though she wouldn't admit it to a soul.

"I'll just have to run," Mrs. Crowley said, clearly

distracted by the insistent peal of the doorbell. "Mind
that you're careful now, Hallie. We have no idea
where that Brock boy's been or what he's been up
to."

Hallie replaced the receiver. Not only did she intend to be careful, she intended to avoid him. Parkdale's bad boy had always spelled *Danger* with a cap-
ital *D*. Especially for Hallie. He had a dark, go-to-hell
look about him—an intensity that made her heart
pound and her palms sweat. Just as oil and water
didn't mix, neither did Cody Brock and Hallie Fortune.

CODY SHIFTED AMY in his arms and tried jiggling her
when she continued to whimper. "It's okay, baby.
Daddy didn't mean to scare you."

The door lock had been rusted from weather and
disuse. His patience only hanging on by a thread and
with a hungry, tired baby to contend with, he hadn't
felt like driving back to town to hunt up a locksmith.
It wasn't the first time he'd busted a window, but it
made him feel rotten that he'd scared Amy.

He looked around the old Victorian home he hadn't
been back to in fifteen years. He'd called ahead to
have the electricity turned on, but that was about the
extent of the house's welcome. Hell, what had he expected? The smell of baking bread and chocolate chip
cookies? Those days were gone. Wasted. His own
fault.

"It's just you and me, kid."

He smoothed the soft black curls on Amy's small

head and rubbed her back. Glancing down, he was once again awestruck by the solemn little girl in his arms. She stared at him with unblinking eyes. Icy blue eyes. Like his own. Eyes that seemed to say, "I've got your number, bud. You don't know a darn thing about babies." And she would be right. He'd only become aware of her existence three weeks ago. It had been three weeks of eye-opening hell, weary soul-searching and scary decisions.

He wanted so much for this little girl, to give her the world, to do the right thing by her. An impersonal apartment in Chicago hadn't struck him as the proper environment to raise a child, so he'd done the only thing he knew to do. He'd come home to the house he'd inherited yet shied away from, back to the close-knit town he'd tried his damnedest to get kicked out of as a kid. Would the good folks of Parkdale, Illinois welcome him with open arms? That remained to be seen.

Memories swamped him as he made his way from the kitchen to the living room. Everything looked the same, except somebody had come in and tossed sheets over all the furniture. Probably his sister.

His *sister*. Hell!

Cody's arm tightened around Amy in a grip that had the little girl protesting. "Sorry, sweetheart. You're so little, I keep forgetting I have to be careful." Her iridescent blue eyes still tracked him like a magnet. He felt exposed, as if she could read his every thought. He had an idea she wouldn't much care for his thoughts about his sister.

A master at hiding his emotions, Cody grinned, trying to inject confidence in the look. The kid knew he was a fraud. She poked out her lip and the whimper turned into a pitiful, quiet little cry.

"Okay," he said. "Action. That's what we need. We'll get busy and do something." He whipped the sheet off the couch and cringed at the dust that stirred the stale air. Amy hushed up, her little eyes going round. "See, baby. This could be fun. Here, you give it a try." He moved to the reclining chair and bent down. "Grab it and give it a yank."

She stuck a thumb in her drooling mouth and curled her other hand more tightly in his collar.

"No?" he asked.

"Ba ba," Amy mumbled around her thumb.

"Bottle. Right. I should have thought of that. It's here somewhere." He snatched up the diaper bag and Amy nearly toppled out of his arms as she bent double, reaching for his pants.

"Oh, silly Daddy. I forgot where I put it, didn't I pumpkin. But the groceries are still in the car. Here, you sit right there and wait while Daddy goes and gets them." He plopped her on the couch but had only taken two hurried steps before a piercing wail stopped him.

"Oh, Amy." He forced his jaw to relax, forced the clenched muscles in his stomach to unknot. "I'll be right back. Two seconds. I promise. Just to the car and back."

Tears tracked down her chubby cheeks, breaking his heart. He retraced his steps and swung her up in his arms, feeling totally inept. "How do people do this?" he muttered, gently patting her on the back as he strode out the front door and yanked open the hatchback of the Blazer. "A person needs four hands for this sort of thing."

He had to straddle the motorcycle trailer hitched to the truck in order to reach the grocery bags. With Amy's arms gripping his shoulders, her head tucked into the curve of his neck, hauling the shopping bags out required dexterity and a good sense of balance. Lucky for him, he possessed both.

He cast a longing look at the motorcycle, wishing he could turn back the clock, back to the blessed days of freedom when he could climb on that bike and just take off with no particular destination in mind.

Guilt slammed into him at the thought. He had a huge responsibility now. Amelia Dawn Brock, to be exact. And he intended to take that responsibility very seriously. Even if he did end up withering away from lack of sleep.

Cody pressed his lips against Amy's forehead in a quick kiss of apology for his selfish thoughts. "Maybe we'll see if they make baby seats for Harleys. How about that, huh?"

Amy didn't respond. He hadn't expected her to.

Balancing the baby in one arm and two paper bags under the other, Cody retraced his steps to the house. A can of shaving cream fell into the bed of petunias—somebody had been watering them, he noted—and a Hungry-Man frozen dinner landed with a splat close beside it. Strewing groceries all along the front walk seemed to get Amy's attention and she made the whole situation worse by craning her neck, leaning to the side and pointing. Cody nearly dropped her.

"Oops," she whispered around the ever present thumb in her mouth.

"Oops, did you say? Is that a new word?" He grinned as her rosy lips opened into a fleeting smile. "Hey, oops is a good word." At almost a year old, Amy's vocabulary seemed limited. Not that Cody knew what the vocabulary of an eleven-month-old should be. Still, he worried that his little girl was way too solemn.

He also worried that his fatherhood abilities were seriously lacking. With one arm around Amy, he unloaded diapers, animal crackers, baby powder, toothpaste, frozen dinners and beer. As if to taunt him for being an idiot, she held out her empty bottle.

"Ah, jeez, Amy. I forgot to buy the damned milk."

EVEN-TEMPERED, Hallie wrote in her spiral notebook. Yes, that was a major requirement, definitely a pro. It should have a weight of at least five points more.

Easygoing. Nonargumentative. She chewed the end of her pencil. Tim Levine's Pro column was adding up nicely. But didn't those three descriptions pretty much hold the same meaning? Perhaps she ought to erase a few of the pro points. It was sort of like stuffing the ballot box to keep adding pluses for the same category. She intended to go about her husband hunt in a logical manner, but she owed it to herself to be strictly fair about it.

With the eraser poised in indecision, Hallie jumped when a set of impatient knuckles rapped at her front door. She chided herself for the way her heart pounded. It's probably just Mr. Delong, she thought, coming to see if she had the lowdown on the riffraff who just arrived in the neighborhood. George Delong was always grumbling about the state of the town and its changes. "Nothing but a bunch of damned yuppies," he'd say, "moving in and changing things when they was perfectly fine before."

She wondered if he'd call Cody Brock a yuppie. Not likely.

When she pulled open the front door, Hallie had to coach herself to take a breath. It wasn't Mr. Delong standing on her porch. It was Cody Brock.

"Well, I'll be damned," he drawled. "I didn't expect to see you here, Slick."

Slick. He'd called her that as a kid. It had always thrilled her. It still did. "Who did you expect?"

"Your folks, I suppose." His expression never altered—Cody didn't give himself away easily—and his eyes remained locked with hers.

"They're divorced," Hallie said. The nervous chuckle that escaped seemed inappropriate. "On their twenty-fifth anniversary."

"Sorry."

"Don't be. They should've made that decision twenty-four years earlier. I'm sure you remember the fighting." She saw his gaze shift to her mouth and knew exactly what he was thinking, what he was remembering. She wasn't about to take that particular trip down memory lane with him.

"Anyway," she said hastily, "Mom took off on a cruise and Dad took up with a younger woman. I got the house."

The little girl in his arms lifted her head from his shoulder. Coal black hair and eerie, pale blue eyes. Just like her daddy's. The sight of Cody Brock cradling a baby girl in his arms would take some getting used to.

"Cute baby."

His gaze still hadn't wavered from her face. "Hungry baby," he corrected. "I...uh, could I borrow some milk?" He held up a plastic bottle decorated with pink elephants wearing tutus and toe shoes. The little girl made a grab for it. "It's empty, Amy," he said softly. "Hang on a sec." His stoic expression slipped, giving Hallie a glimpse of a stark uncertainty she'd never expected to see on this man's face. "I went shopping, but I forgot the formula."

"No sweat. It happens to the best of us. Come on in." She couldn't believe she'd left him standing on the doorstep with a hungry baby while she'd waxed on about the outcome of her parents' disastrous marriage. But his unwavering stare had made her uneasy. It suggested the baby wasn't the only one who was hungry.

"So, is your wife due soon?"

"No wife."

She paused, glancing back over her shoulder, first

at Cody, then the baby. Her heart bumped against her chest, annoying her. "Divorced?"

"Never married."

The quiet, matter-of-fact statement jolted her. Hallie gave herself points for not stumbling. It didn't matter a bit that Cody Brock was unattached. And it didn't matter that he was handsome as sin or that just a single, searing look from those pale blue eyes could whip her pulse into overdrive quicker than a shot of adrenaline.

He was not on her list of candidates for a potential mate. She wanted a safe man, an easy man, a man whose emotions would not clash with hers.

Cody Brock made her feel volatile, like a volcano on the verge of erupting. For too many pain-filled years, she'd witnessed those same emotions between her parents. They'd started out with sexual passion that had burned too hot, too fast, drowning itself in a pattern of explosive bitterness.

She didn't want to repeat her parents' mistakes. No. She wanted something completely different for herself, for her life. From the time she'd first laid eyes on Cody Brock back when she was twelve years old, something in his brooding eyes told her that if she let him in, he'd shake up her peaceful world and she'd never be the same again.

As she passed the dinette table, Hallie picked up her spiral notebook and shoved it into a kitchen drawer. She wasn't taking any chances that he might see what was on that paper—and ask about it.

"So, where've you been all these years, Cody?"

"Living, you mean?"

"Mmm." Opening the refrigerator, she took out a carton of milk. There was an extra half gallon. She'd send one of them home with him. It would get him by until he could get to the store for the proper formula.

"Chicago for the last few years. Before that, here and there."

"Here and there? Sounds mysterious. What, were you in jail?"

"Hell of a question, Slick."

She heard the low tension in his voice, a voice that scraped along her nerves and shot her libido to a dangerous high. "Sorry. That was rude. Can't blame a girl for wondering, though. It's been a long time. And you were always a hellion, Cody Brock." She tempered her words with a smile.

"Yeah. I guess you'd remember me that way. Not jail, though. The Marines."

Her hand jerked, the stream of milk missing the mouth of the bottle. "Desert Storm?" She snatched a rag and wiped the mess before it could drip on the floor.

"Yeah."

So that's where he'd been when his folks had died. She'd thought it just awful that he hadn't shown up for their funeral. Dear Lord, he *couldn't* show up. He was halfway around the world.

She finished pouring milk into the bottle, capped it and attempted to pass it to Cody. Two chubby hands reached out instead.

Smiling, Hallie ran her fingers over Amy's baby soft curls. Recently, just the touch of a baby, the special smell of one would make her ache. She almost asked Cody if she could hold his little girl, just to feel that warm tiny body next to her heart. She held her peace, though. Someday, her time would come. She would have children of her own to hold, to love, to nurture. A tiny person who would need her, yes, but more important, a person who would love her.

She watched as Cody settled Amy more comfortably in his arms, marveled at the gentle expression that came over his face. He didn't appear to be in any hurry to leave.

"Would you, uh, like to sit down?"

He nodded and hooked the leg of the dinette chair with his foot, scooting it out to accommodate both himself and the child.

"Where's her mother, Cody?" Hallie asked softly.

He didn't take his eyes off his daughter. And neither did the daughter take her eyes off the father. It was a moving sight, almost as if they were in a stubborn battle, each taking the other's measure. "Off to find fame and fortune in Hollywood, I suppose."

Hallie frowned. "You said you weren't married. Did you live with her?"

"No." He looked up then, piercing her with those brooding eyes. "Shall I lower your opinion of me even further by telling you that I didn't even know about Amy until three weeks ago? I slept with her mother once, on a night when I was torn up with grief and drunker than I should have been."

The nurse in her immediately wanted to object to the dangers of such behavior. But the turbulence in Cody's eyes stopped her. It appeared he'd chastised himself plenty. "Oh" was all she said.

"Did I shock you, Slick?"

"Of course not." What did he think she was? Some kind of prude?

He grinned, cocking one dark brow in silent challenge.

"All right. Your point," she conceded. "I suppose I did have a fleeting thought about the irresponsibility of drinking to excess with little thought for the consequences. I told you once you needed a keeper."

"And I asked you if you'd be mine."

"You were teasing me," she said.

Several beats of silence hung in the air. "Was I?"

The way he drawled the question raised her blood pressure. It also annoyed her...and exhilarated her.

"Stop trying to bait me, Cody, or I won't do the neighborly thing by sending that extra carton of milk I have in the fridge home with you."

He grinned. "I've missed you, Slick."

Hallie laughed. "Yeah, I'm sure. Like a bad disease. You used to deliberately try to scare me off."

"Sometimes. I succeeded, too."

"Did not."

His brow cocked, reminding her of a dark James Dean. "The bad boy and the do-gooder," he mused. "So, what are you doing with your life now?"

"I'm a nurse." What had he meant by that bad boy, do-gooder comment?

"I bet you're good. You always were compassionate."

For some reason it bugged her that he'd pegged her so accurately, both then and now. Never mind that it was true. "You barely knew me, Cody."

The look he gave her held enough wattage to sizzle. It ought to be illegal for one man to project that much sensuality, especially while holding an innocent baby. His voice, when he responded was low and intense, with just the barest hint of a warning.

"Oh, yes I did. I knew you very well, Hallie Fortune."

Chapter Two

Cody knew he'd shaken her. Her expressions had always been easy to read. He decided to press a little more. Just to see where it got him. "I was right, you know."

"About what?"

"That day I found you crying out by the lake, I told you you'd turn out to be a beauty. I just hadn't anticipated how beautiful."

He remembered the skinny tomboy. Recalled how he'd teased her, acted tough around her to deliberately scare her off. She'd always been the peacemaker, the good little girl with big brown puppy dog eyes that made a guy feel worshiped and damned full of himself. That had been his first reason for steering clear of Hallie Fortune.

The second had come the day before he'd shipped out to the Marines. She'd been fifteen. He'd ridden up on his motorcycle and caught her crying. Her parents had fought. Again. As she'd done countless times, she'd run off down to the lake, to a special spot under an old elm tree.

He'd gotten into the habit of watching her, mostly when he heard shouts coming from the house. His vow to maintain distance had crumbled that day and he'd given in to his need to just sit with her, absorb some of the goodness that at happier times simply radiated from her. Hallie Fortune wasn't the type of girl who should be crying alone.

True to form, she'd spit at him like an angry kitten, rejecting his attempt to console her. That was a side of her that only surfaced when *they* were together. With everyone else in town, Hallie was all sweetness and smiles, even-tempered in a way that made him want to tease her, test her—dared him to ruffle her composure.

He'd kissed her that day, back when she was fifteen. He'd only meant to soothe, but his intentions had boomeranged and smacked him square in the heart. And in his libido.

She'd scared the hell out of him. Not because she was jailbait, but because of what she made him feel. He hadn't experienced that depth of longing before or since.

But the image he'd carried around with him, through some of his darkest days, didn't begin to compare with the woman sitting across from him at the sunny yellow dinette table.

Long blond hair that spilled halfway down her back framed her smooth oval face. Her brown eyes were wide, the type of eyes that could draw you in and make you want to stay a while. A man could spend a lot of time just on that face. And her body. When she'd opened the door earlier, he'd felt as if somebody had just punched him in the gut. A pair of tight jeans would snag him every time.

His gaze settled on her pouty bottom lip.

"Cody Brock," she snapped. "Don't you dare pull that smooth, tough guy routine on me. You might have intimidated me when I was fifteen, but I'm all grown up now."

"Yes, indeed you are." Fifteen years hadn't quenched his desire to bait her. "And it wasn't my intent to intimidate."

"No?"

"No. As a matter of fact, my ego's feeling fairly battered that you didn't recognize my silent signals of seduction."

Her eyes widened, as if she'd just pushed a rewind button, weighed the words and tones once again, and come up with the elusive answer. It both surprised and aggravated him when she laughed.

"Give me a break. You're holding a baby in your arms. Besides, I'm not your type and you're certainly not mine."

"Ouch. Didn't anybody ever tell you the male ego's a fragile thing?"

She snorted. "I think yours will survive."

"Hmm. Debatable. So, what's your type?"

"Somebody safe," she answered right away. "Even-tempered. A guy who doesn't argue at every turn—" She stopped, glaring at him. "Why are you shaking your head?"

"That's not your type, Slick."

"No? Well, since you're such a man of the world, why don't you tell me what is."

"You need a guy who'll stimulate you, keep you on your toes, ruffle those prissy feathers. A guy who'll shake that good-girl foundation you're so intent on showing the world."

"Oh, for Pete's sake. You haven't laid eyes on me in fifteen years and just like that—" she snapped her fingers "—you think you know me?"

He shrugged. "I recognize passion when I see it."

"A relationship doesn't boil down to just sex."

"I wasn't necessarily talking about sex. But if you want to, we can."

Hallie ignored the bait. "Okay. Let's talk about this other emotion. I'm an expert on the subject. My parents were perfect examples of what happens when two intense people try to make a go of it. Hot sex becomes humdrum and all that's left is the passion of bitterness." She shook her head. "Watching a destructive pattern for twenty-five years is a surefire way to show a person what they want and what they *don't* want for their life."

He watched her for a long moment, as if he were trying to figure out an aggravating puzzle. Then he grinned. "Shame on any guy who lets hot sex become humdrum."

She should have been shocked, sitting here at the kitchen table, talking about sex with a bad boy holding a sleeping baby in his arms. Instead, she felt alive, her blood humming just below the surface, heating her in a way that made her feel sassy and invincible. And happier than she'd felt in a long time.

She groaned and bit her lip to keep from laughing. "I can't believe we're discussing my parents' sex life. This strikes me as a darn good time to change the subject." She glanced down at the little girl in his arms. "Looks like Amy's out."

"Not for long." Every trace of teasing drained right out of his tone. "I can't seem to get her on any type of a schedule." He lightly touched the baby's fingers, then jerked back in alarm when they twitched. For several seconds, he seemed to hold his breath.

"She scares me, Hallie. The way she looks at me with those solemn eyes. It's as if she can see my soul and hasn't decided yet if I'm a guy she's willing to trust."

Hallie wondered if he realized his own eyes had a similar impact on people. "It's just a matter of the two of you getting used to each other. You said it's only been three weeks, but there's a definite bond there."

"I'm not used to somebody relying on me like this, of not having any time to call my own." His expression suddenly brightened with hope. "I don't suppose you'd be a pal and help me out?"

Hallie shook her head. "What, do I have *sucker* written across my forehead? I'm on vacation, Cody. Amy's an angel, but my days are full." Full of scorecards and pros and cons on husband candidates.

"Sorry," he said. "I shouldn't have asked. She's my responsibility. It's just that…"

"What? Being a single parent's hard?"

"Yeah. How do people do it? How do you get anything done?"

"Put her in day care?" she suggested.

"No." He was adamant on that. "I've just found her. I'm not ready to give her over to a stranger for eight hours a day."

"You were willing to give her over to me."

"Not for eight hours. And you're not a stranger."

"Okay. Plan B then. Put her in a walker. Let her follow you around. Or, when that's not feasible, put her in a playpen with plenty of stimulating toys. Work when she sleeps."

"I don't own a walker or a playpen and she *never* sleeps."

"She's sleeping now."

"No. She's still sucking. See, her lips are moving."

"Reflex," Hallie said, reaching over to take the bottle.

"Don't!" he whispered.

"No need to whisper now. She's slept right through our conversation." The bottle came out of Amy's mouth with a smack of suction. Her eyes remained closed, her body limp.

"How'd you do that?" He was clearly awed, like a kid witnessing magic for the first time.

"Practice. I'm a nurse, remember? And now's a good time to get some of those things done that you wanted to do," she advised.

His gaze lifted. An emotion akin to panic flared in

his eyes, but was quickly masked. "In other words, I'm keeping you from something."

In all honesty, she could spend the rest of the day just looking at him. But Tim was due to stop by any minute now. Tim was safe, easygoing and quiet. According to her chart, the marriage scale was tipped heaviest in his direction. So far, he'd earned twelve out of fourteen points. An excellent record.

She smiled gently. "I'm glad you're back, Cody. This is a good, solid town to raise a child." She got up and retrieved the carton of milk from the refrigerator. "This'll hold you until you can get to the store."

Halfway through the living room, the doorbell pealed. Amy flung her arms out, startled. Cody froze, jiggling her and holding his breath. She immediately settled right back into sleep.

"See there," Hallie said with approval. "That wasn't so bad." She opened the front door to Tim Levine. He was a bank manager, one of those young, up-and-coming types. Nice looking, tall and rangy. He wore three-piece suits on weekdays and preppy casual clothes on weekends. Today was a casual day, knit shirt and slacks. They were going to a picnic sponsored by the Parkdale National Bank.

"Sorry," Tim said. *Jingle, clink. Jingle, clink.* The coins in his pocket tinkled as he habitually shifted them through his fingers. "I didn't know you had company."

When Hallie held out the door for him, he stepped

in and extended his hand to Cody. "Tim Levine. Parkdale National."

Cody nodded tersely but didn't make a move to accept the handshake. Never mind that his hands were full with Amy and the carton of milk. He could at least verbally state the obvious.

Hallie raised her brow at the deliberate rudeness. Tim, on the other hand, didn't even appear to notice the slight. Hallie jumped into the breach.

"Tim, this is Cody Brock. He's from next door. He just stopped by to borrow some milk and…" She suddenly realized what she was doing and shut her mouth. Why the hell did she feel the need to explain Cody's presence in her home? Tim didn't appear to care one way or the other.

Cody, Hallie noted, wore an expression that would make anyone with a good sense of self-preservation take a step back. She studied him a little closer. The rigid set of his body reminded her of a dog who expected to have his bone stolen. It fairly shouted both a warning and an impolite curiosity. If she didn't know better, she'd think he was jealous. Which was perfectly ridiculous.

"Well," Hallie said, feeling awkward. "I'm ready to go, Tim. I just need to grab my purse." For a minute, she thought she was going to have to give Cody a shove.

Then he inclined his head once. "Levine. Hallie." He turned and strode off the porch and across the lawns.

"Seems like a decent guy," Tim said absently, jingling the change in his pocket.

Hallie forced her gaze from Cody's retreating back and made a concentrated effort not to let her jaw drop. *Decent?* Had she and Tim been standing in the same room? Surely she hadn't blinked and missed something. Like a shred of common courtesy?

If she had any doubts before, she didn't now. Even at thirty-three Cody Brock was still moody and unpredictable. Tim, on the other hand, was safe and polite and had handled that horribly awkward moment beautifully.

She didn't bother to examine the notion that awkwardness hadn't even occurred to Tim. He trusted her, she told herself. And he was sure enough of himself that he wouldn't be intimidated by a bad boy.

His lack of emotion was the very trait she admired most.

She made a mental note to chalk up another pro on her chart in favor of Tim Levine—that's thirteen out of fourteen. Now she just needed to devise a reason to borrow his change. *All* of his change. The constant jingle, clink of coins was about to drive her nuts. Maybe she'd put a jar by the front door and make him empty his pockets when he came in. She'd tell him it was a fund she'd started for the ladies auxiliary or something.

CODY DIDN'T KNOW why he was so uptight. It was only natural that Hallie would have other men in her life. He was a little surprised she wasn't already married with a passel of kids. Apparently she hadn't found the right sort of wimpy guy who wouldn't argue with her, he thought sarcastically.

Did she actually think that banker guy could make her happy? Tim Levine, she'd said. Hell, the jerk hadn't even reacted to finding another man in Hallie's house. And Cody had gone out of his way to be rude. He hadn't intended to do it. The behavior had just happened. So he'd gone with it, checking to see if old Timmy boy would rise to the occasion.

"Parkdale National," Cody mimicked nastily. As if his job defined him or something. *Idiot* defined him better. There hadn't even been a hint of that macho sort of measuring two men did now and again in the presence of a coveted woman. No possessive step to drape an arm around her shoulders, no silent signals warning away trespassers. Was the guy blind or just dead below the belt?

And that change-jingling thing the guy did. Damn, it was annoying. Levine gave the impression he was laid-back, yet the coin habit told a different story. It indicated anxiety, discontent, impatience.

What the hell kind of guy would be impatient while looking at Hallie Fortune? The woman was a knockout curvy blonde, for God's sake. Any red-blooded man with a single healthy hormone would give up courtside Bulls' seats just to sit and look at her for hours on end, to dream about her, imagine that sultry voice whispering in his ear, her smooth hands touching his skin, her lips pressed against his....

Cody swore and raked his hands through his hair. He'd been too long without a woman.

Still, if Hallie had been *his* woman he wouldn't have taken another guy's presence in stride that way. He'd have stepped right up to her, body touching close, and casually brushed his lips against her neck. His palm would have rested at the slight curve of her waist, his thumb damned near brushing the sweet swell at the underside of her breast, plain enough that even a simpleton would get the picture and heed the warning.

"*Hell* of an imagination, Brock," he said aloud, then held his breath when the sound of his voice disturbed Amy. "Please don't wake up, baby," he whispered. "Daddy's worn-out."

Amy threw her little arm up over her head and sprawled out like a limp frog. Cody relaxed and inched his finger over to stroke the delicate skin of one chubby arm. In three short weeks, this baby girl had become so precious to him. Granted, she still scared him half to death, and he didn't know the first thing about what was right for a kid her age, but when she wrapped those chubby arms around his neck, or laid her tiny head against his chest with such utter trust, it made him feel damned near invincible.

He propped a mountain of pillows around her so she wouldn't roll off the low sofa bed, then removed his shirt and lay down beside her.

He wanted to sleep for ten hours straight. Reality and three weeks of experience told him he'd probably only get two.

EVEN THOUGH SHE WAS on vacation, Hallie rarely slept past six. She was up and dressed in shorts and a sleeveless blouse by seven, a cup of coffee and her spiral notebook in front of her on the dinette table.

Bank picnic with Tim, she wrote. In the Con column she jotted down the word, *Dull,* then chewed on the end of her pen, considering the description. To be fair, that wasn't exactly Tim's fault. The picnic was a company thing. Naturally most of the people there would talk about mortgage rates and fiscal predictions. She circled the word and figured she'd come back to it later.

Under Pro she listed: Clean car, Steak house restaurant, Punctual, Chaste kiss, Conversation...

She gave the last entry some thought. They hadn't actually talked about anything profound or stimulating. As a matter of fact, she couldn't accurately recall *what* they'd discussed.

Cody, on the other hand, had definitely engaged her in conversation. She remembered every stimulating word he'd said. Now, how in the world had that thought slipped in? she wondered. Shocked, she realized she'd just written Cody's name on her chart. She started to scribble it out. He wasn't a candidate for her list. Then she thought better of it.

Just to prove how wrong he was for her, that he had absolutely none of the qualifications she sought in a man, Hallie went ahead and listed the two headings by his name.

Pro: Good father.

"Not enough facts for a firm opinion," she decided, drawing a line through it.

Pro: Nice butt.

"Oh, for Pete's sake!" That one got two lines through it. Best to start with the easy stuff.

Con: Moody. Volatile. Heartthrob. Dangerous. Passionate. She underlined the last one several times, then tossed the pen on the table. What the heck was she doing? Losing it, she decided, plain and simple. "Get a grip, Hallie," she muttered. "*Please,* get a grip!"

Cody Brock didn't belong on her list. If she hadn't learned her lesson at fifteen, she'd certainly wised up after that disastrous college fling. A fling she'd jumped into because the guy had reminded her so much of Cody.

Shoving back the chair, Hallie stood and marched over to the sink to dump her cold coffee. She rinsed the cup, filled it with tap water and carefully watered the African violets in the kitchen window.

A movement caught her eye and she paused, squinting. Sure enough, the doggy door over at Cody's swung out a few inches. She gazed at the leaves on the pear tree. They ruffled, but not enough to indicate a strong breeze.

Had Cody also brought an animal with him?

A squirrel scampered down the bark of the pear tree, paused, bushy tail high, then darted across the yard. No pet there. The darned squirrels were a nuisance.

The doggy door swung out again.

Curious, Hallie went to the kitchen door and stepped outside. The humidity had already reached a sticky eighty-five percent and it promised to get worse. The weather service predicted a late summer heat wave. That didn't bode well for some of the elderly in town whose homes weren't equipped with air-conditioning.

When she looked back at Cody's house, Hallie was stunned to see a naked baby crawl right out that doggy door.

"Oh, Cody," she said with a laugh. "That little girl's gonna give you a run for your money."

Expecting to see Cody burst out the back door in hot pursuit, Hallie stayed put in her own yard. Amy plopped down on her bare butt—apparently it was still too early for the cement to have heated up yet—and gave the swinging door a curious shove, obviously pleased with herself.

The kitchen door itself remained shut and Hallie frowned. Hadn't he realized yet that his kid was loose?

Amy rolled from her chubby bottom onto all fours and started out across the lawn, heading straight for a fallen pear with bees buzzing around its sticky fruit.

Hallie took off at a run.

She scooped up Amy just in the nick of time.

"You little stinker. You're a smart one, aren't you."

Amy stuck her thumb in her drooling mouth and grinned.

"See that pear?" Hallie asked, pointing to draw

Amy's attention. "It's got bad old bees on it. Buzzy things. They sting little girls." She made a buzzing sound and Amy removed her thumb long enough to clap. Babies were so precious first thing in the morning, all sleepy and warm, so very curious about the dawn of a new day.

Hallie buried her face in Amy's neck, breathing in the sweet baby smell of her. "Where's that daddy of yours, huh?"

Cody still hadn't appeared. Hallie had been right to cross off the "good father" notation. The jury was definitely still out on that issue.

She checked the back door and found it locked. Shifting Amy more securely on her hip, she knocked politely on the door.

And waited.

She looked down at Amy whose curious blue gaze clung like a magnet. It gave Hallie a funny feeling, as if this small child were taking a walk right through every thought in her brain, yet reserving judgment for another time.

"You've got eyes just like your daddy's," Hallie commented. The word *daddy* got Amy's attention and she looked back at the door.

"Yeah. I'm wondering the same thing. Where the heck is he?" This time Hallie pounded on the wood frame, earning herself a set of sore knuckles for her trouble.

Muttering unkind words about Cody's poor sense of parental responsibility, she raised her arm to try again and froze as the door was suddenly jerked open.

Half-awake, shirtless and barefoot, Cody Brock glared at her. The power of those piercing blue eyes jarred, leaving her speechless and trembling with sensations so vibrant they hurt.

He had the body of a god, tall and tough, muscled in all the right places. Broad shoulders tapered to a lean, hard waist. The raven hair on his chest didn't overpower. It only enhanced a virility that made a woman long to ease up against and stay for a good long time.

"Hallie?" he said, bringing her out of her sexual trance. "Amy? What…? Oh, God!"

The real panic in his voice and deep blue eyes made Hallie pause. This guy needed help, she decided.

Her help.

But right now *she* needed some distance, an hour or two to examine these dizzying, molten sensations that were racing through her system at a bewildering rate. Sensations she might not have recognized or known what to do with at fifteen, but certainly understood now.

Dangerous sensations she could never, ever allow herself to give in to again.

"Hardware store," Hallie advised, thrusting the naked baby into his arms. "You need a lock for that doggy door."

Turning, she fled across the lawn, wondering if she'd ever again be able to draw a decent breath. The sight of Cody Brock, half-naked, had just set her safe world spinning on a shaky axis.

Chapter Three

Several hours later, Hallie figured she had herself well under control. She was smart enough to realize she was breaking her own vow, but if ever there was a person in need, it was Cody Brock.

For the second time that morning, she knocked on his door—this time, the front one. His response to the summons was a lot quicker than the first time around.

"I've come to ask a favor," she said when he appeared, looming over her in a manner that had her taking a step back. Thank heavens he'd put on a shirt!

"Shoot."

"I'd like to borrow Amy."

"Define *borrow*," he suggested suspiciously. Perhaps it was fanciful, but she thought she detected a hint of residual panic in his eyes.

"This is my day to deliver meals-on-wheels. It's only for about an hour, maybe longer depending on who's in the mood to talk. It occurred to me that a baby would be the perfect morale booster for some of my regulars. They don't get a lot of visitors. It'd probably be good for Amy, too."

For a minute she wondered if he'd been listening. His eyes made a slow pass over her body, loitering on her sleeveless top, spending an inordinate amount of time on the top three buttons she'd left undone.

She was fairly certain she could speak, but there was no point in taking a chance. She cleared her throat instead.

His gaze snapped back to hers, frank and assessing. "Okay. I'll get my keys."

Her mind had gone sluggish under the power of that long look. It took her a second before his words registered. He was already halfway across the living room.

"Wait! That's not necessary. I can just take the car seat out of your Blazer and transfer it to mine." Why the *hell* did her voice sound so breathy?

He turned back, pinning her with an unreadable look. "I'm going with you."

"You weren't invited."

His raven brows flattened at her blunt statement. "You think I'd trust my baby girl to just anybody?"

"Oh, for Pete's sake. That baby girl escaped out the doggy door this morning. Naked. While you were sleeping, I might add. Do you really want to debate which one of us is more trustworthy?"

"Do you want to take her with you or not?" he asked tersely.

"Yes, I want to take her with me. Jeez. I thought I was doing you a favor here. You said you needed help and—"

"Slick?"

"What?" She felt a quick ripple of unease when he called her that. It usually meant he was going to tease her...or make her heart bleed.

"The fact that Amy got out without me knowing about it shook me up. Maybe I'm not ready to let her out of my sight again so soon."

"Oh." The contrition she saw in his eyes and heard in his voice took the wind right out of her sails. *Make her heart bleed,* she decided. "In that case, maybe you could *both* use a pick-me-up."

He flashed her a smoky smile. "I knew I could count on your compassion."

Hallie had a sneaking suspicion she'd just been had.

"Why don't you come on in while I get the diaper bag ready."

"Sure."

The house was a disaster, Hallie noted. Some of the furniture was still draped in sheets. She spied a wadded up diaper between the easy chair and end table. With a shake of her head, she bent to pick it up, wincing at the strong smell of ammonia. She'd have to remind Cody to alternate Amy's bottles with plenty of water.

The kitchen was even worse then the living room. It did a fairly credible imitation of *Animal House.* Frozen dinners half-eaten, congealed leftovers and cracker crumbs littered the sink and counters. Good heavens.

He hadn't put any of the groceries away. Apparently he had no idea what cupboards were designed for. A bag of chips had busted open, raining ranch-flavored taco chips all over the tile floor. To give him his due, Hallie figured he'd just gotten sidetracked, would have every intention of sweeping up the mess.

Poor guy. It appeared he really was out of his element.

Her sense of orderliness offended, Hallie shoved open the kitchen window to let in fresh air, scraped the largest part of the mess into the trash bin—along with the diaper—and ran a soapy rag over the tile countertop, scooping up mushy cereal and spilled milk.

Amy's high-pitched squeal and Cody's deep rumble of laughter drew Hallie out of the kitchen. She wandered back through the rooms to see if he needed help, but a stack of storyboards on a drawing table snagged her attention.

Curious, Hallie flipped through them. *Pals,* she read. Her gaze darted to the boldly scrawled signature in the bottom right corner. *C. Brock.*

"Well, I'll be," she whispered. If she'd known this was Cody's line of work, she'd have found more time to read the newspaper, especially the comics.

The cartoon featured two guys wearing Marine fatigues. Harlan and Darby. Harlan wore a leather jacket over the fatigues. The other, Darby, had wild, curly hair and freckles and held an open book. Sort of like Opie from Mayberry meets the Fonz, she decided, flipping through the stack of drawings.

In each of the dialogue bubbles above the cartoons, it appeared that the hoodlum, Harlan, had a penchant for asking profound questions about life. The nerdy one, Darby, would scratch his head, then suddenly appear in the next frame with a book on the subject...and a credible answer.

"I see you've met Darby and Harlan."

Startled, Hallie whirled around, her face heating at being caught snooping.

Cody stood in the doorway with Amy in his arms. He'd dressed the little girl in pink overalls and sandals. Clipped to one of her dark curls on top of her head was a pink barrette shaped like a teddy bear. The image of Cody's large, capable hands positioning that barrette just so made everything within Hallie go soft.

Father and daughter were staring at her with identical wary blue eyes.

Hallie cleared her throat. "I'm impressed." She indicated the storyboards with a sweep of her hand. "I never thought to look in the comics for life's answers."

Cody shrugged. "You could just as easily find those answers in the encyclopedia."

"Maybe." Hallie had an idea she could find out a lot about the real Cody Brock if she studied this comic strip from its inception to the present. "I'm glad to see you're using your talent for drawing."

"It's fairly easy to draw variations on the same guys day after day."

"No need for modesty, Cody. I've seen some of the things you've sketched." She glanced back at the drawings. "My guess is that Harlan is you. Who's the other guy?"

"What makes you think this strip is autobiographical?"

Hallie raised a brow and grinned. "The leather jacket's a dead giveaway."

"You always were a smarty-pants. The other guy's a Marine buddy."

He stepped close, crowding her. Hallie's eyes widened as he leaned into her. She knew a sexual come-on when it hit her over the head. What made it worse, though, was her desire to take him up on it.

The scent of soap clung to him, teasing her with erotic visions of naked shoulders and a rock-hard chest dusted with raven hair, water sluicing over smooth muscles...

She closed her eyes, felt him shift. "You ready to go call on the old folks, Slick?"

His breath tickled her ear and her eyes sprang open. He'd only been reaching around her to straighten his drawings. Obviously the subject of the Marine buddy was closed.

And so was the subject of whether or not he'd been about to kiss her, Hallie lectured herself. "Sure," she said, surprised that her vocal cords worked.

"Fine. We'll take my Blazer. It'll be easier than switching the car seat."

"Suit yourself," Hallie agreed. "But I'll drive."

HALLIE HADN'T CHANGED that much over the years, Cody realized, except in appearance. Watching the sway of her hips under white shorts was about to drive him wild. In deference to the heat, she had her hair tied up in a loose ponytail. Several platinum strands had escaped their ribbon and clung to her damp neck.

She still had the sweet personality of her youth. A natural with kids and the elderly. Everyone she touched benefited from her presence. Including him, Cody mused.

He watched, fascinated, as she drew Edna Fitzpatrick into conversation, resting her fingertips on the woman's frail wrist. To the recipient of that touch it was kindness, a communication of warmth and caring. But Hallie's brand of touch served more than one purpose. Cody knew she was actually monitoring pulse rates.

"How are you feeling today, Edna?"

"Oh, 'bout the same, honey. You're such a good girl to take the time to come all the way out here for me."

"Now, Edna, you know I love visiting with you. I've brought some friends with me today." She reached for Cody's hand and drew him closer.

Each time she touched him, he felt the connection jolt clear up his arm. It was getting tougher by the minute to be in the same room with this woman. She was dynamite to look at, to watch…to dream about. He kept having to remind himself that they were in the presence of an elderly woman. And that he was holding his baby daughter in his arms.

Obeying Hallie's slight tug, Cody squatted next to

the overstuffed chair and rested Amy on his knee. "How do you do, Miz Fitzpatrick? I'm Cody Brock."

"Brock," she repeated, her birdlike hands reaching out to stroke his face. The woman was blind, he realized with a start. "Gerald and Miranda's boy," she said with a sad bob of her head.

"Yes, ma'am." His gaze collided with Hallie's. She seemed to want to reach out to him, but Edna Fitzpatrick's hand was still cupping his cheek.

"I was real sorry to hear about your folks. They were good people. Miranda would come to see me pretty near every day. She was always talkin' 'bout her Cody. A proud mama she was."

Cody didn't bother to debate the proud mama statement. The woman was obviously being polite. He'd given his folks a rough time, deliberately—much to his regret. There was no way to atone for that now. They were gone. Had been for six years now.

Cody had to clear his throat before any words would come out. "Thank you."

The bony hand patted along his neck and shoulder and came to rest on Amy's head. Skin as translucent as rice paper stretched into a wide, wrinkled smile. "And who's this little lamb?"

"This is Amy," Hallie said. "Cody's baby daughter."

"A baby girl," she said reverently. "Well, isn't that wonderful. Great-grandbabies would have been a pure joy for Miranda."

"Granddaughter," Hallie corrected.

"Yes, of course." Edna patted Cody's knee, then

clapped her hands and held them out in Amy's direction. "Can I hold you, sugar?"

To Cody's astonishment, Amy wriggled right up on Edna's lap, exploring the age-lined face with fingers wet with drool. Edna laughed and hugged and laughed some more.

When Cody glanced over at Hallie, her brown eyes were liquid with emotion. He felt a tug at his own heart and had to look away. Who would have thought that one little baby would make such a difference in an old woman's day?

An old woman who obviously knew all the dark secrets of Cody's past. At least the ones prior to Gerald and Miranda Brock's deaths.

SINCE MRS. FITZPATRICK was the last meals-on-wheels delivery on Hallie's route, they spent a little longer there than with the others. Amy, bless her heart, had a wonderful time assisting the sight-impaired lady with her meal. It didn't do for Cody to object to the mess. Edna only shooed him away.

Now, stepping back out into the muggy afternoon heat, Cody cradled a tired Amy against his shoulder. A semi had taken up a good portion of the curbside when they'd arrived, so the Blazer was parked a block away.

They walked down the tree-shaded sidewalk past seventy-year-old homes with well-tended lawns. Children played in front yard sprinklers and darted past on bikes. It was a peaceful town, a good town to raise kids.

Cody was just congratulating himself on his decision to settle here when they were nearly mowed down by a kamikaze car with a little old lady at the wheel, and another in the passenger seat.

Snatching Hallie by the waist, he yanked her to him, feeling her pulse race beneath his fingertips. He frowned at the menace in the old Buick who'd bumped clear over the curb and crossed one driveway to get to the other, coming to a halt with a bone-jarring screech.

"You okay?" he asked.

Hallie nodded, her lips pressed together to hold back a grin. "Fine, and you?"

"The jury's still out. Remind me to go have my heart checked soon, though." He shifted his gaze back to the '56 sedan, taking a moment to appreciate the classic. "Hell, no wonder they missed their driveway. Neither one of them can see over the dash."

"Actually," Hallie said, "they're in their own driveway. Just took a little detour to get there. Miss Ida?" she called. "Miss Lila? Are you two okay?"

"Right as rain," Ida called back, hopping out of the car with a spryness that belied her age. She halted, shoving her spectacles back on her nose and pinning Cody with a hawklike look. "Young man. Why do you look so familiar? What is your name?" she demanded.

Cody remembered that tone. And that look. It hadn't boded well in sophomore English. It made him sweat now. "Uh, Cody Brock, Miss Ida."

"Well, I'll be dogged. Sister, it's Cody Brock."

"I've got a set of eyes," Lila snapped, holding a hand over her bosom and glaring at her sister. "A damned sight better than yours, I'd say. You've run over that sweet girl Crissy Metz's flower garden again."

"Oh, I did not. And when does Crissy Metz have time to tend flowers anyway, I'd like to know. That poor girl works night and day at the steak house."

"You did so run over her flower garden," Lila argued. "And I certainly know how hard that girl works. She lives right next door, you old hag."

Hallie couldn't prevent the laugh that escaped. Cody's whole hair line had shifted when Lila called Ida a hag. She linked her arm with his and headed back toward the Blazer. The sisters, caught up in their bickering, didn't seem to notice they'd left.

"Sobering thought that those two taught us in school, isn't it?"

"Hell, I was just feeling smug for moving back to such a safe neighborhood, and now I have to worry about retired schoolteachers driving on the curb."

Hallie laughed again and patted his shoulder. "Be thankful they don't live on *our* street."

Cody felt a jolt of emotion he couldn't quite put a name to. Her enticing lips were stretched wide, bringing animation to her beautiful face. He had to lengthen his stride just to keep up with her. Hallie did everything with gusto and passion, even something as simple as walking.

She adored people, animals and life, went out of her way to bring a spark of happiness to everybody's day. Including his own. Everything Hallie touched flourished, from flowers to old ladies.

Yeah, he decided, he liked the way she'd said *our* street. It linked them somehow. A bond that was starting to look pretty damned good.

WHEN THEY GOT HOME, Hallie volunteered to change Amy's diaper and dispatched Cody to the kitchen for lemonade.

It was while he was chasing stray ice cubes that he ran across her chart. At least it looked like a chart. He wasn't sure and frankly, it was none of his business.

Still, the ice cube had landed right on top of the pages. Anybody'd take a quick glance, he rationalized.

Tim Levine. Brian Hollister.

He frowned and immediately dismissed every rationalization he'd thought of about reading something that was none of his business. Hell, it was sitting in plain sight. Besides, she'd looked at *his* drawings without permission.

Out of curiosity, he compared the comments under the two names. Pros and Cons, he read. Hollister, an accountant according to Hallie's notes, hadn't done too bad, but the positives were definitely stacked in favor of the coin jangler.

Cody snorted and pulled up a chair. He flipped the page to see if there was more and froze.

His name was on the list.

The single line through *Good father* affronted him.

The double lines through *Nice butt* brought a grin. The other five—all in the negative column—shot his blood pressure up and down and up again so fast he swore.

"Passion is a *bad* thing?" he muttered. "Ah, hell." He finally understood exactly what he was looking at.

It appeared that Hallie Fortune was in the market for a husband, a sensible, safe, passion*less* husband...and Cody wasn't even in the running.

His grip tightened on the melting ice cube in his hand, leaving a telltale splotch on the spiral notebook. A muscle ticked in his jaw.

"We'll just see about that, Slick."

Chapter Four

Amy fussed for the better part of the next day, so Cody finally gave up on completing his latest story-board. Besides, every time he tried for just the right expression on Harlan's face, it didn't fit the tone of the strip. Instead of concentrating on the interaction between the "pals," he ended up doodling, surprised when the new sketches took on a different twist.

The cartoon of the baby with drooping diapers made him grin. The nurse in a minidress on roller skates carrying a boxed lunch made his heart pound.

Maybe this was a sign. Harlan and Darby were about to have their world shook up by a do-gooder and a baby.

Cody tossed his pen aside and straightened his drafting table. The more he thought about these new characters who'd been born out of the blue, the more he liked the idea. After all, his own life had been turned upside down by a baby and a sexy nurse. Why shouldn't Harlan and Darby's life reflect the same fate?

Ideas poured into his brain, but he couldn't do a

damned thing about them. Amy needed his attention right now.

He scooped her up off the floor. "You're gnawing on those fingers again, squirt." He pulled her thumb out of her mouth, which sparked a brief tussle. "You're going to hurt yourself, baby. Just look at this thumb." He held up the angry red appendage for inspection.

Amy whimpered and Cody frowned. "Here, let Daddy see what's going on in there." He stuck his finger in her mouth and she bit down. Her gums were swollen. Something sharp was piercing the surface. A new tooth.

He was thrilled by this latest discovery. Apparently, Amy didn't share his enthusiasm. Her solemn blue eyes widened when he applied pressure and her face crumpled. He snatched his hand back immediately.

"Oh, no. Daddy's sorry. Don't cry. You know how Daddy hates it when you cry." He jiggled her, wondering what to do next. "You poor little thing. No wonder you're chewing. Here, have your finger back." He lifted her hand back up to her mouth. "Just chew all you want. If you do damage, we'll see a plastic surgeon or something."

Carrying her into the kitchen, he turned on the tap to wash his hands. He should have thought to do this *before* he'd stuck his fingers in the baby's mouth.

"I need an owner's manual for you, kid." Or a certain sexy nurse to give him a few pointers.

The fiery sun had sunk low behind the elm trees,

but the muggy, oppressive heat still prevailed. They needed rain. Hallie's flowers needed rain.

As if the thought had conjured her, he glanced out the kitchen window. Sure enough, she was tending the bed of impatiens next to the driveway.

He took a moment to appreciate the tight fit of her shorts. Her platinum hair was pulled into a ponytail again today. He wished she'd let it loose to flow down her back but decided that probably wouldn't be too comfortable in this heat.

Amy craned sideways to splash in the running tap water and Cody almost lost his hold on her. Especially since he was so preoccupied with the guy who'd just pulled up in Hallie's driveway in a midsize economy car.

That'd be the accountant, Cody decided. He shut off the tap and grabbed a towel to absently dry Amy's hands. She began to wriggle, so he set her on the floor and headed for the front door, chuckling as Amy scrambled after him on all fours. Pushing open the screen door, he stepped onto the porch.

"Hey, Slick?"

Both Hallie and her gentleman caller turned. The accountant frowned. At least this guy reacted—not like the preppy banker whom he'd taken to calling the "suit" and who wouldn't recognize rude if it bit him in the butt.

"Amy's getting teeth," he yelled.

Hallie grinned. "Good for her."

Now it was Cody's turn to frown. That wasn't the answer he was looking for. "Well? What do I do?"

"Same thing you did when the others came in."

"I didn't have her then. She *came* with four teeth!"

Amy crawled out between his legs and attacked his shoelaces. Before she could make a knot that would take him twenty minutes to undo, he swung her into his arms and headed off across the lawn, secretly pleased for an excuse to break up Hallie's little tête-à-tête with the stuffy accountant. Besides, it was demoralizing to yell across the yard like this. It left too much room for rejection, for her to turn her back on him in favor of the new guy who'd just driven up.

Cody operated on instincts and first impressions. His first impression of the banker had been weak. This guy struck him as stuffy. God help him, he was going to have to save Hallie from herself. Scorecards, for crying out loud.

He stopped in front of the two and held out his hand to the other man. He hadn't missed Hallie's censure the last time he'd been rude to one of her men friends. "Cody Brock," he said.

"Brian Hollister. Accountant." The guy's handshake was firm enough. But why the hell did everybody in this town feel the need to qualify their name with a job title?

Satisfied that he'd done the polite thing, Cody dismissed Brian and turned to Hallie.

"She's in pain." He'd predicted Hallie wouldn't be able to resist Amy. She cooed and neatly eased her finger in Amy's mouth. Cody was a little put out that the baby didn't object with so much as a peep.

Instead, the pint-size traitor grinned, showing off four front baby teeth that were already fully formed.

"Yep," Hallie said to the baby. "There's another tooth in there. Aren't you a big girl?"

"Well?" Cody prompted.

"Well, what?"

Cody frowned and took another look at the accountant. Was she so preoccupied that she'd forgotten the question? At least this Brian character had enough male sense to step closer. Cody followed suit, his shoulder brushing Hallie's. "What do I do?" he repeated.

"Teething is perfectly natural, Cody. Do you have liquid Tylenol or Orajel?"

"No." He noticed that her eyes widened when his hip bumped hers, that her pupils were dilating. Good. "What's Orajel?"

"It numbs the gums."

"I've got whisky." He'd used that whisky to numb more than his gums. He'd anesthetized his brain. And that particular error in judgment had resulted in Amy.

"Alcohol poisoning is not an option."

He frowned at the reproach in her voice. "I wasn't going to put it in her bottle. So, do you have any of this gel stuff?"

"No, but Brian and I were just headed for the store to get a couple of steaks for dinner. Why don't I pick up some up for you."

"Steaks?"

"No, silly. Tylenol and Orajel."

"I wouldn't want to be a bother." His voice

sounded strained, even to his own ears. He couldn't remember anybody ever calling him silly—there weren't many who'd have the nerve. He was highly trained in the techniques of deadly force, for crying out loud, skilled at inspiring both fear and respect in a company of Marine soldiers.

He was also damned good at strategical planning and maneuvers, he thought with a fair amount of amusement, and the idea of throwing a monkey wrench in Hallie's plans with another man was just too good to pass up.

"I'll just go with you to the store. That way you can make sure I don't get the wrong stuff."

"Go with…?"

"Amy and I will take our own car," he assured. "We won't intrude. Just point us in the right direction and then forget about us. You won't even know we're there." Unless you're blind, he thought, giving her a smile that would have done Red Riding Hood's wolf proud.

NOT INTRUDE? Hallie thought. Not know he was there? Cody's presence in the grocery store caused reactions like a movie star among their midst. Everyone was curious. And when he turned up the wattage on that smile, the ladies, young and old, flocked.

Hallie all but hissed. She barely looked at the steaks she tossed into the basket and rudely ignored Brian when he questioned the lack of marble in the T-bone.

That's because she'd just caught sight of Cody, not five feet away, on the baby aisle.

Tearing open a package of Orajel.

Before she could caution him otherwise, he'd stuck some on his finger and put it in Amy's mouth.

The little girl wailed.

Cody froze.

"Oh, mean daddy. Shame on daddy! Don't cry baby. Here." He shoved a bottle in her mouth and pulled her little cheek against his hard belly, petting and stroking in his attempt to soothe.

Hallie, for the first time in her life, felt jealous of a baby.

She wondered what it would feel like to have her own face pressed to that hard chest, her lips tasting and teasing, his large, capable hands running over her body, offering encouragement....

"Uh, Hallie?"

"What?" She jumped at the sound of Brian's voice. She'd forgotten he was even there.

"Shouldn't we be moving along? It's getting late. I've got an early start in the morning and I still have to run Aunt Lucinda over to Lila and Ida's for their poker party."

"Oh! Yes, of course."

As she pushed her cart down the frozen food aisle, a thought struck her. "I'll be right back, Brian."

Cody was still in the same spot. Amy was happy once more, a bottle held in one hand, the thumb of the other in her mouth. She appeared thoroughly enchanted with the haphazard way Cody was tossing stuff into the cart.

"You don't need everything on the shelf, Cody."

"You never know. Hey, check out this spoon. It's coated." He tossed it into the basket among the growing pile. "Drives me nuts to hear teeth scraping on metal. Where's your date?"

"Over in frozen foods," she answered, distracted. The power of those devastating blue eyes jarred her. She tore her gaze away and reached for a teething ring, coaching herself to breath. It annoyed her that her hands trembled. "You need one of these. Keep it in the freezer, then let her chew on it. The cold will numb the gums."

"You might have told me sooner before I stuck that jelly stuff in her mouth. I think she's still mad at me."

"You'll catch on." Hallie laughed and patted him on the arm, feeling smug in the face of his masculine helplessness. But the minute her palm touched his biceps, she knew she'd made a tactical error. Heat scorched up her arm, sensitizing nerve endings that were already humming.

She jerked her hand back and glanced away, looking everywhere but at the fire in his assessing blue eyes.

"I, uh...think you can take it from here." She started to move away.

"Wait," he said softly, his voice holding the barest edge of panic...and something else she couldn't identify. "I still need the pain killer stuff. Walk with me. Just a few minutes more."

"Brian's waiting."

"I need you, Hallie. Please?"

There was that word again. *Need.* It bothered her, but she couldn't resist. So Hallie found herself strolling down the grocery aisles with Cody, discussing the salt content and nutritional value of the various foods. They made it to the produce section before Amy started to fuss.

Cody, ever resourceful, grabbed three shiny red apples and began an impromptu juggling act.

Amy was impressed.

So was Hallie.

Smooth muscles flexed with each toss of the fruit. Riveted, Hallie stared, catching a glimpse of a tattoo on his upper arm as the sleeve of his Marine T-shirt shifted.

Something dangerous and thrilling rippled through her. Cody was a man who could handle himself in any situation. A protector. A man who wore absolute confidence like a layer of skin.

She saw his gaze shift toward the electronic doors of the store, yet he never dropped a single apple.

"It appears your accountant got tired of waiting."

Hallie whipped around in time to see Brian stomp out the front doors.

"Oh, no! I forgot all about him." She frowned at the stiff set of his shoulders. He was pouting. Not a good sign. She'd have to remember to add a few negatives to Brian's column. *Pouts. Leaves me in the gro-*

cery store to walk home. Sticks me with the bill for steaks....

"The bill," she said suddenly. "Darn it! He was supposed to buy dinner. I didn't bring my checkbook."

She'd been stunned to see Brian walk out the door, now she was angry. Of all the low-down, rotten, childish things to do. Any other woman with a backbone would march right out after him, grab him by the collar of his knit polo shirt with the two little golf clubs over the breast pocket and demand an explanation for his rudeness—never mind that *she'd* forgotten about *him*.

The rebel inside Hallie could vividly picture doing this. But her peace-at-all-costs temperament dismissed the notion almost as quickly as it surfaced.

"Want me to go deck him for you?" Cody asked, never missing a lick of his apple toss.

"That's all you'd need to cement your reputation. Get in a public brawl and land yourself in jail."

"You're right. If *I* hit him, it won't satisfy your need for vindication. So, we'll do a drive-by and you can let the air out of his tires. I'll be the lookout."

She realized he was teasing. The devilish sparkle in his deep blue eyes was a gentle admonishment that she took herself too seriously.

She reached out and snatched an apple from midtoss. The other two came to a halt in his large palms. "This is all your fault, you know."

"Sorry."

He didn't sound sorry at all. In fact, he looked entirely too pleased with himself. He started to stack the apples among the neat rows of shiny fruit.

"Don't you dare put those back. Now that you've bruised them, you've got to buy them."

He turned to her, very slowly, two perfectly shaped apples cradled in his palms, his thumbs stroking the smooth skin as if they were a woman's delicate breasts.

"My touch never bruises, Slick," he said softly.

His eyes said so much more than words, holding her with a challenge that made her nervous and edgy and much too aware of him as a man.

An exciting, *dangerous* man.

Rather than allowing herself to be drawn in to his sensuality, Hallie changed the subject. "I'd better go find my abandoned cart and put the stuff back."

"No need for that. We'll just stick your things in with mine."

"No. I can't let you buy my groceries."

"Was that the deal? He'd spring for the food and you'd cook?"

"Something like that." Said out loud, it didn't sound like such a hot deal.

"I'll offer you a better one. I'll buy *and* cook. We'll toss in something mushy for the kid here and make it a threesome."

"*You* can cook?"

"Don't sound so shocked. We ex-Marines are handy to have around."

"I'm going to take you up on that offer simply because the idea of you in the kitchen is too intriguing to pass up.'' Besides, it appeared she was free for the night anyway.

''I can think of a whole list of ways to intrigue you, Slick. And not all of them involve the kitchen.''

The sexual taunt in his deep voice thrilled her and scared her to death. Maybe this wasn't such a good idea after all.

As if he'd read her thoughts and her reserve, he placed a finger under her chin until her gaze met his.

''There are plenty of other places besides the bedroom.''

Her jaw dropped, hitting his finger. ''Who said anything about—''

''You did.''

''I did not!''

''Those big brown eyes will give you away every time.''

Hallie jerked back. If he kept touching her she'd end up in a puddle smack in the middle of Jefferson's Market. ''In your dreams, ace.''

''You're already in my dreams.''

''Cody Brock! What's gotten into you?''

He grinned.

''Never mind! Don't answer that.''

''I like teasing you, Slick. Brings out that fire I remember so well.''

Teasing her. She should have known. Same thing as fifteen years ago—except the subject matter had a more X-rated slant to it. Friends, she reminded herself.

''Fire will burn you, Cody.'' Oh, how she wished

that wasn't true, but she had firsthand experience to support the belief.

"Not if you tend it right. Where's your cart?"

"Over in frozen foods," she answered absently, her mind snagged on vivid images of Cody tending a fire...a sexual fire.

"Well, let's get it before the stuff melts."

"Cody—"

"Hey. Don't back out on me now. We've got a deal. Besides, your number-crunching date has left you without wheels. Not only do I cook a mean steak, I'm a hell of a chauffeur."

CODY POKED at the charcoal and accepted the plate of seasoned steaks Hallie handed him.

"You've got to take pity on me, Slick. It won't take long to shop for a crib and playpen and a few baby clothes. An hour, tops. Besides, you saw what happened in the grocery store."

"Yes. You opened the merchandise before paying for it. Serves you right that Amy caused a scene." The idea of going shopping with Cody again held a certain appeal. An appeal that she had no business looking forward to.

"The apple juggling was a nice touch, though. Did you notice that Jeanie Atkins ran over Lisa Garmetti with her shopping cart?"

He shot her a narrowed look. "No, I missed that one."

"Didn't you date Jeanie back in school?"

His mouth kicked up in that damned bad-boy grin

that made her pulse skitter. "Yeah. I did. She had a thing for the underside of the bleachers at football games. How is old Jeanie, anyway?"

Hallie couldn't find any good reason for the pang of jealousy that clutched at her heart. "On her second divorce," she said smugly. "Lives off Treemer Street."

"Behind the drive-in?"

"The drive-in's closed now. They used it as a swap meet for a while, but that went bust, too. Now it's just an abandoned piece of cracked asphalt with a few broken speaker poles. Signal Land Company submitted plans to the city a while back for a strip mall, but pulled out of the deal because the area's become so run down."

"A lot's changed since I've been gone."

"Yes. How come you never came back, Cody?"

His wide shoulders lifted in a shrug. "I was stationed in Okinawa for a while, then in California. The timing never seemed to work out."

"Did your folks visit you?"

"A couple of times. They liked Disneyland."

He flipped the steaks on the grill and used the spatula to wave away the billow of white smoke. She saw his gaze shift across the yard, to his parents' house that he now owned, saw a muscle tick in his square jaw.

As always, the subject of his parents made him clam up. There was hurt there, a wound that festered, unable or unwilling to heal. Hallie couldn't figure it. Gerald and Miranda Brock had been ideal parents:

loving, nurturing, stable. They didn't fight. And Cody had led them on a merry chase.

"I'm having a hard time reconciling the contrasting sides of you, Cody. The one when you lived here in Parkdale and the one of you as a Marine...and now a father."

"What's to reconcile? We're talking fifteen years."

"And you've changed?"

He shrugged. "Looks are often deceiving, Slick."

"Yes. But to coin another cliché, actions speak louder than words."

"Actions then, or now?" He glanced at her, and at the little girl she held in her arms, his dark brow raised. "What you're dancing around here is you want to know what made me tick back in high school?"

"Yes." And what made him tick now.

"I carved out a hotheaded, troublemaker image for myself as a kid. The tough guy thing stuck, even when I didn't want it to. Guys wanted to fight me. It got to where I'd walk into a room already watching my back, always scanning the surroundings for potential trouble. Trouble had a way of finding me."

"And that time Miranda had to bail you out of jail on Mother's Day? That's pretty bad, Cody. What did you do anyway?"

"Nothing as shocking as you're obviously conjuring."

"So set my mind at ease."

When he turned the full force of his attention on her, Hallie felt her blood sizzle. For several heartbeats, she became lost in his eyes, unable to look away. "Do I make you uneasy, Slick?"

Heavens, yes. His voice had lowered, deepened, sending chills down her spine. Chills in eighty degree weather. "Don't sidetrack me, Cody. What did you do?"

"How come you didn't ask me this back then?"

"Because most of the time you acted like a jerk to me." Then there was the other half who was so sweet it hurt. "Besides, it wouldn't have been polite."

"And you were always the polite one. Lose your cordiality along the way?"

"Oh, for Pete's sake. If you don't want to answer the question, just say so."

"I've got no problem with answering. I've never met a woman yet who wasn't intrigued by a rebel." The slight dimple in his cheek deepened as his mouth quirked.

"Now, don't go letting that ego of yours get out of hand."

"Ego? You mean that masculine thing you've always taken such great care to step on?"

"I have not!"

"You'd be surprised, Slick," he muttered. "I got sent to juvie for joyriding in a stolen car."

Hallie's eyes widened. She was both appalled and intrigued, like a spectator at a racing event, appreciating the nerve and skill of the drivers, yet looking for the gore. "You stole a car?"

"No. I didn't steal the car."

"Oh."

He chuckled at the disappointment in her tone. "I was hanging with some of my buddies. We got hungry and decided to go to Burger Boy. Phil Havlin said he'd drive. He was sixteen so I assumed he had a license. Phil was screwing around and weaving all over the road, which earned us the attention of the law. The cops hit the lights and Phil took off like we were in a Vette instead of a 4-cylinder bug."

"He tried to outrun the police?"

"Yeah."

"Whose car was it?"

"His sister's. She didn't know he'd taken it and she reported it missing. I got hauled in as an accessory."

"How anticlimactic. You're burning those steaks, by the way. I thought you said you could cook."

"I can. I didn't say anything about barbecuing, though. The menu choice was yours."

"Brian's," she corrected absently, resting her cheek against the soft curls of Amy's dark hair. "What's the difference?"

"When you cook on the stove, you can control the flame. Charcoal's a turkey shoot. Either the coals go out and you end up with a raw cow, or they're so hot you get beef jerky." He scooped the steaks off the grill.

"I like beef jerky."

The smile that slowly lifted his lips made her breath catch in her throat.

"And I like an agreeable woman." The look he turned on her made her want to flee for her life. Yet she felt paralyzed, unable to move as he reached out, the tips of his fingers barely brushing the bangs that had fallen over her temple. It was a whisper of a touch, yet it packed the power to send her blood pressure soaring. She nearly groaned when he withdrew his hand and treated Amy to the same tender touch.

"I also like the way you look holding my daughter. It's a sight I could get used to."

The statement whipped through Hallie like a winter blizzard, freezing her on the spot.

She couldn't allow his touch or his words to affect her like this. She had an agenda for her future, plans that were in the final stages of completion.

And Cody Brock wasn't part of those plans.

Chapter Five

"Think you can lay her down without waking her?" Cody whispered. Propped in Hallie's lap, Amy's head was lolling to the side, looking entirely too uncomfortable in Cody's opinion.

Hallie nodded and stood, shifting Amy's weight against her shoulder.

"Good. I'll do the dishes."

"My kind of guy," Hallie said with a sassy smile.

He watched as she left the room, her bare feet hardly making a sound against the wood floor.

Her kind of guy? Not according to that point system thing she'd devised, he wasn't. That thought had him scowling at the dishes as he rinsed plates and stacked them in the dishwasher. The silver tray that had held the meat slipped out of his soapy hand and landed on the countertop with a horrendous clatter.

Cody froze, praying Amy wouldn't wake. When he didn't hear an angry wail, he exhaled. Would he ever get used to having a baby around the house? The profound sense of relief he felt when Amy slept bothered him.

Sometimes he wondered if he was wishing her life away—in slumber.

He'd commanded an entire company of Marine soldiers, yet one tiny little girl shot his confidence to hell.

The sun finally slipped below the horizon. With night, came the awakening of crickets and frogs and the call of a night bird as it took flight over the lake. Fireflies flickered in the bushes outside the kitchen window.

Closing the dishwasher, Cody crossed his ankles and leaned against the countertop as he waited for the coffee to brew.

The steaks had indeed been a cross between beef jerky and steak tartare—charred to a crisp on the outside and undercooked inside. He had an idea he'd be raiding the refrigerator a few hours from now. But at least Hallie had spent the evening with him—instead of with that other candidate, Brian what's-his-name.

He reached in the cabinet for mugs, grinning at the set with sunflowers on them. The whole kitchen was done in a blue-and-white checkered pattern with bright yellow sunflowers. The sunflower motif was everywhere—sunflower babies, wooden dolls with sunflower dresses and bows in their hair, sunflower ducks and chickens and cows. Teapots and knickknacks.

Even that infamous chart he'd run across was decorated with the sunny flowers.

The coffeepot signaled its readiness with a shrill

beep. The scent of cinnamon wafted up as he poured the dark brew into two cups.

"I think she's out for the night," Hallie said, entering the room and moving to the sink to wash her hands.

"You've definitely got a way with her that I obviously don't."

She frowned. He'd noticed that same expression outside when he'd commented on how good Amy looked in her arms. For some reason, the mention of his daughter in conjunction with Hallie bothered her. He wondered about that.

"I'm used to children," she said. "I work with them every day."

"Poking shots in their heinies and sticking tongue depressors down their throats?" Unable to resist, he reached over and slipped the elastic band from her hair, drawing in a breath as silky platinum hair spilled down her back.

She shut off the tap water. He saw her shoulders lift as she inhaled deeply. She wasn't unaffected by him, yet she held a part of herself back. He had an urge to shake her up, make her want him as badly as he wanted her.

He cocked a brow when she sidestepped him.

"I don't just give shots and look in children's throats."

"What else do you do?"

"Just about everything the pediatrician does. I'm a nurse practitioner."

"I'm impressed. You've done well for yourself over the years."

"I make a comfortable living."

"And this house with all the sunflower babies in it. Your folks letting you live here?"

"No. I bought it from Mom and Dad." She straightened the apron on one of the wooden sunflower dolls, a doll that stood about waist high.

"You bought it?"

"Don't sound so shocked. I told you I get a pretty decent salary. And I'm obsessive about savings accounts. Anyway, like their marriage, my parent's divorce was ugly. They fought bitterly over every stick of furniture and the market value of the property. I liked the neighborhood and the floor plan of this house, I had great credit and a good-size down payment just moldering in the bank. So I made them an offer that we all found reasonable, held an auction and liquidated the furniture. They split the money and everybody ended up happy."

"Still stepping in between them?"

Her shoulders lifted. "It's a hard habit to break."

"So where are they now?"

"Mom took her half of the proceeds and bought a condo in Florida and took a cruise. I don't know what Dad did with his money. He took off with a waitress half his age. I haven't heard from him in over a year."

"That's got to be rough on you."

"Not really. It took a lot out of me to watch what they did to each other. The fighting. It's actually kind of nice now. Peaceful."

"And you're looking for peace."

"Yes."

"Boring."

She glanced at him sharply. "It is not. I've got friends, my job, the charity stuff in town—"

"But no husband."

For a minute, Hallie was too stunned to answer. She finally found her voice. "No," she said softly. "Not yet."

The ticking of the kitchen clock seemed amplified in the sudden silence.

"Can I ask you something?"

"If I say no, will that stop you?"

"Probably not. What's with that scorecard thing you're doing?"

As bombshells went, that one was a doozy, heading straight for her midsection, where it exploded.

"Were you snooping in my things?" Indignation colored her words yet she felt her body flush with embarrassment. She'd wondered about the wet smudge on the pages. Had he flipped the page and seen *his* name? What the devil had she written about him anyway? She couldn't remember, and she couldn't very well go check with him staring at her this way.

"I wasn't snooping. It was sitting there in plain sight. So I looked."

"Well, you shouldn't have."

"Well, I did," he declared. "So what's the deal?"

Hallie shifted her weight and wondered if she should answer honestly. Then she figured it couldn't hurt. If he understood her mission, maybe he'd back off and leave her to it. Having him turn on that powerful charm every time she so much as looked at him was causing some serious interference with her plans.

"I'll be thirty in a couple weeks," she said. "I want babies and I want happiness…and I'm old-fashioned enough to want marriage in order to have those things. That's what I want. What I *don't* want is to lead the type of life my parents did, nor will I put a child through what I grew up with. That's why I have lists, Cody. To make sure my decision is the right one. My decision for a husband."

"Isn't that a little cold-blooded?"

"No. It's safe."

"What about passion? Does the *suit* turn you on?"

"The suit?"

"The banker."

She rolled her eyes. "His name is Tim."

"Whatever. Does he turn you on, Hallie?"

"That's none of your business."

"Just what I figured."

"What?" She didn't trust that tone.

"He doesn't do it for you."

"I didn't say that."

"You didn't have to."

Cody thought he was so smart. Never mind that he was right. She needed to put a stop to this conversation before it got entirely out of hand. "Well, you're wrong. Tim's as hot as they come."

"Liar," he said softly, taking a step closer. "I bet you haven't even slept with him."

And he'd win that bet, but Hallie wasn't about to admit it. She held up a hand palm out. "Stay right where you are, Cody Brock."

He ignored her command, advancing like a panther stalking its prey, taking her wrist in his hand and moving it aside. "You're looking for guarantees, Slick. There are no guarantees in life."

"All the more reason to hedge my bets." With the sink at her back and Cody surrounding her, she had nowhere to run.

"And you think some chart with a point system is going to do that?" There was an edge to his voice, a razor sharpness she didn't understand.

"Maybe."

"Well, add this to your point system."

Before Hallie could prepare, he slid his arms around her waist and pulled her up against his body with gentle force. The touch of his lips was part caress, part demand, a demand that Hallie met without thought and with a fervor that stunned her. The power of the kiss whipped through her, instantly wiping away any hope of sanity.

His tongue swept her lips, asking for and receiving entrance. She didn't stop to think about the message behind his kiss, a kiss that had turned hot and hard and sexy. It was the kiss of a bad boy, a thorough foray that warned of danger, a forbidden taste of ecstasy.

He wedged his thigh between her legs, pinning her up against the kitchen cabinets. Fire swept a path along her nerve endings. The sure pressure of his leg at the juncture of her thighs sent starbursts skyrocketing behind her lids. She felt dizzy with pleasure, her entire body awash with such exquisite, mind-shattering sensations she wanted to scream.

It was too much. Hallie fought the feelings, the intensity, the passion. If she gave up control, she'd shatter, never be the same again. She'd yearn for that passion for the rest of her life, even knowing it would destroy her.

She pushed against his shoulders. The pressure between her thighs eased as he leaned slightly away, but the throbbing remained. Her breath came in shallow gulps. "Cody, I can't do this."

"Why not?" His fingers tightened at her waist.

"It's not what I want." She drew in an unsteady breath. "I'm dating someone else."

"*Two* someone elses," he reminded.

Hallie sighed. "That's my choice."

He looked at her, his expression unreadable. There was heat in his gaze, and desire. Those were obvious. But beyond the sexual, she couldn't tell what he was thinking.

Finally he stepped back, leaving her bereft at the loss of sensation and chastising herself for missing it.

She couldn't allow herself to get used to Cody's brand of passion. She just couldn't.

"Why did you kiss me?" she asked.

"Call it an experiment."

That irritated her. His hot blue gaze still probed, making her feel as if he could see clear through to her soul. "Did you get the results you were after?"

"Yeah," he muttered. "It's just like I figured. You scared me at fifteen. You terrify me now."

CODY HADN'T ASKED her to go shopping with him after all, which was just as well, Hallie decided. That kiss had left her more shaken than she cared to admit. It had been two days and she still couldn't get the taste of him to fade. He aroused her fantasies, stimulated a sexual curiosity she hadn't thought about in years, if ever. He challenged her on a level that made her nervous and edgy.

She felt that edginess now and knew she needed to get out of the house.

Muggy heat surrounded her as she made her way across the street carrying the chicken casserole she'd baked early that morning. Hazel Crowley had sprained her ankle last week and although it was on the mend, Hallie worried that the woman wasn't eating properly. And Lord knows, Hazel would be the last person to ask for a helping hand.

Hazel waved from her perch in the white wicker chair on the porch. "You've been cooking again," Hazel said. "That usually means you've got heavy stuff on your mind."

"No, it doesn't," Hallie argued sweetly. "It just means that I've got a busy schedule. If I want to eat anything decent, I need to prepare it ahead of time. Lucky for you I got carried away with the boiled chicken. You get a casserole out of it."

"And I'll enjoy every bite. Stick it in the fridge for me, would you, hon? Then come on out here and join me. Grab a soda on your way, too. Keeping an eye on the neighborhood's thirsty work.''

Hallie laughed and did as she was told. Instead of soda, though, she poured iced tea in two tall glasses and returned to the porch, handing one of the tumblers to Hazel.

It was just her luck to see Cody the instant she sat down. He came around the corner, pushing Amy in a brand-new stroller. He'd made a good choice. The stroller was top of the line. She felt a slight pang at the dent he'd obviously made in his checkbook. But that was Cody's problem, she reminded herself.

"Mighty fine-lookin' man," Hazel commented.

Hallie raised a brow. "Are you speaking of Mr. Delong?" George was out in his front lawn with the garden hose, overwatering as usual.

"Gawd, no. That old coot's 'bout as ugly as a garfish. Snappy as one, too. No matter what I say, the man disagrees with me. Tell him the sky's blue and he'll swear it's pink."

"Then why do you give him the time of day?"

"Because it feels good to spark a little with a man. Even at my age." Hazel cackled. "Don't tell him I said so, though."

"My lips are sealed."

"And so are your female hormones if you ask me. I'm an old lady, Hallie, and I'm darn near drooling over that handsome young man pushing the stroller. Why in the world aren't you after him?"

"You know I'm dating other people."

"Oh, pshaw. Always room for one more rooster in the pen, I say."

"Hazel, you're shocking me."

"I doubt that. You should go for him, dearie. Just look how good he fits in those jeans."

"Shh! Not so loud!" Hallie didn't need any reminders of how he looked in his jeans. She'd dreamed about just that for the past two nights. She saw Cody glance their way and suddenly wished for a hole to open on the porch and swallow her whole.

"That boy seems to have grown up right nice. Appears to be a pretty good daddy, too."

Hazel was fishing for information. That much was obvious. But Hallie had never liked gossip. She'd been the butt of it too many times when her parents had fought. Well-meaning friends and neighbors whispered about that sweet Hallie Fortune having to live in such unstable surroundings. The gossip had embarrassed her, put more pressure on her to try to keep peace in her household. "He cares a great deal for Amy."

"That's plain as the nose on your face. Where's the child's mother?"

"I don't know. I think she more or less abandoned Amy."

"What a pity."

Yes, it was a pity. She saw Amy's little legs kicking against the footrest of the stroller. They'd stopped in Cody's driveway now and he was lifting her out. He tossed the little girl in the air and Hallie sucked in a breath, letting it out slowly as he caught the baby in sure hands. She should have known. Cody would never let somebody fall.

He'd caught Hallie enough times. It seemed whenever her emotions were all over the place, Cody would appear. He hadn't touched her—except for that one time at fifteen—but he'd never let her fall.

The sound of Amy's happy squeal melted Hallie's heart. It appeared Cody's daughter was finally warming up to him.

"How's your ankle holding up?" Hallie asked.

"Almost good as new. I can't believe I stepped in that darn gopher hole. They're making a mess out of my yard. You seen any yet?"

"No. They haven't made it across the street so far. If they mess with my flowers, though, you can be darn sure I'll be knocking on George's door to borrow his gun."

"Land sakes," Hazel laughed. "I never thought of that. I bet George would get a kick out of doing a little target practice in my backyard. I think I just might suggest it."

"Oh, dear." An image of George Delong laying in wait for unsuspecting gophers, gun in hand, flashed in her mind. "What have I started?"

"Actually, you just gave me a good, valid excuse to call on the old grouch." Hazel sipped her tea and rested the icy glass in her lap. "Will you be going to the Founder's Day celebration this weekend?"

"Mmm," Hallie said, distracted. Cody had just set Amy on the seat of the motorcycle, his dark head bent close to her tiny, sweet face, as if he were explaining the workings of the machine in great detail. "You know I love a parade. I haven't missed one yet."

Hallie kept her head turned toward Hazel—it wouldn't do to let Cody know how much his movements interested her—yet her eyes tracked him.

She remembered that bike, the deep-throated rumble of the pipes as he'd rev the engine, remembered wishing he'd take her for a ride. But the only times Cody hadn't ignored her were the times he came to the lake. The times he caught her when her emotions threatened to let her fall.

He'd been her hero. The guy who awed her. A guy who made her yearn to take a walk on the wild side.

A guy who made her want that still, even though she knew it would only bring disaster. She reminded herself of her parents' relationship. And of the bitter experience she'd gone through in college. It was enough to set her back on track.

"Hazel, I've got a while before Brian shows up for dinner. Why don't you show me where you want those new pictures of your grandchildren hung and I'll do it for you."

"Oh, what a sweet girl you are to offer, but Cody did that for me yesterday."

"He did?" Hallie knew she sounded shocked. She couldn't help it. She just didn't picture Cody Brock as the handyman type. "I suppose he hung the café curtains in the kitchen, too?"

"Well no." Hazel sniffed. "I didn't want to take advantage."

"Hazel, sweetie, you couldn't take advantage if

you tried. Come on. I'll hang them up for you. It'll give you a lift to see that pretty lace in the window.'' She stood and helped Hazel to her feet. She had to do something to keep from dwelling on Cody Brock. If she kept sitting here, watching him, she was liable to break her own rule and run right across the street to join him.

CODY KNEW THE INSTANT Hallie went inside Hazel Crowley's house. He'd known they were watching him. He was still new enough in town to be a curiosity. He had an idea, though, that Hazel was doing her best to champion him. And that Hallie was back-pedaling all the way.

He had to grin at that comment about his jeans. Old Hazel Crowley had deliberately raised her voice. And Hallie Fortune was squirming. Good.

He glanced down at Amy who seemed happy enough putting slobber smudges on the shiny black paint of the Harley's gas tank. "If you were a little older, I'd give you a rag and make you wax those fingerprints off my paint, squirt. I don't let just *any-body* mess with my bike.''

She blinked up at him and grinned. "Cikol,'' she whispered.

He felt everything within him go soft when she smiled at him like that. Damn. This little girl was gonna be a heartbreaker when she grew up. He wondered if his own heart would withstand the process. "That's right, baby. Cycle.''

"Fine-lookin' piece of machinery you got there.''

Cody turned as George Delong ambled up, chucking a gnarled finger under Amy's chin. The little girl withdrew, whipping around and reaching for Cody. He lifted her, breathing in her baby scent as she tucked her head in the curve of his neck, peeking shyly at George.

"Hey, now sweet pea," George cooed in a gravely voice. "Don't let an old devil-dog like me scare you." He held out a yellow daisy he'd obviously pilfered from Hallie's yard—she had a whole bunch of them growing next to George's house.

"Get the flower," Cody urged.

Amy blinked up at him, assessing, then treated George to one of her long stares. It was as if her little brain were calculating friend or foe. Finally, she reached out shyly and took the flower. Cody made a swift grab as she automatically shoved it in her mouth.

"Whoa, squirt. Don't eat it. Sniff it." He demonstrated, earning another of those special grins.

"She's a cutie," George said.

"I think so."

"Surprised to see you was a daddy."

"Yeah. Me, too."

George raised one grey, bushy brow, then nodded. "A man sees a lot in the service. Sometimes it makes him do stuff he wouldn't normally do."

Cody looked at the old man sharply. Watery blue eyes met his own. Silent camaraderie passed between them. There were things in a man's soul he didn't dare speak aloud. George Delong held such secrets.

Cody read it in his faraway look. He didn't probe. If George wanted to share the skeletons that haunted his peace, he'd do so in his own time.

"Been a while since you been back to town."

"Yeah."

"Marines, wasn't it?"

Cody nodded. The grapevine was obviously alive and well. Assured that Amy wouldn't put the flower back in her mouth, he released her tiny hand.

"'Bout time a man's man showed up around here. A serviceman." He nodded approvingly. "Durn neighborhood's turning into a yuppie convention, if you ask me. Driving around in those expensive foreign cars, carrying briefcases, spoutin' all that politically correct garbage."

Cody felt amusement tug at his lips. "Nobody's ever accused me of being politically correct."

"Good. You watch yourself, though. Say the wrong thing nowadays and you get tossed in the hoosegow."

"Can't afford that," Cody said. "I've got a kid to think about now."

"Yep. You do. You thinking about courting Hallie?"

The switch in subjects was abrupt. Cody gave himself points for controlling the instinctive jerk that jolted his body. He shrugged, treading carefully. "She's unattached," he said noncommittally.

George snorted. "For the time being, maybe. You seen them fellows been coming around? Never served a day for their country. Got soft hands. Yuppies, the both of them... Although the one drives an American job—probably because the bank gave it to him. I tell you, somebody's got to straighten Hallie out before she goes and makes a damned fool mistake.''

Cody didn't have anything against so-called yuppies, but he did agree with George about Hallie dating the wrong guys. It was a snap opinion, formed from gut instincts. But was *he* the right one to straighten her out? He'd sure as hell like to give it a try.

He remembered kissing her, remembered his emotions spinning out of control so fast he hadn't known which end was up. He didn't like feeling out of control. But neither did he like denying his desires.

Courting Hallie. It had a good feel to it.

''Since I've got your blessings,'' he told George, ''I'll see what I can do.''

''Good. I suspect you're just what that little gal needs.''

He didn't know about that, but he was certainly willing to go along for the ride, to see just where this incendiary desire would lead him.

Chapter Six

While Cody's back was turned, Hallie hurried across the street and slipped in the back door like a coward. He was still out front talking to George. The two were acting as if they'd been lifelong buddies. She snorted. Fat chance. She distinctly remembered Cody busting George Delong's bedroom window back in '79. Now that she thought about it, though, George hadn't thrown a fit like she'd expected him to. Curious.

The phone rang, sidetracking her analysis of Cody's relationship with the neighbors. She plopped on the antique velvet sofa and lifted the instrument from where it sat on the oak end table.

"Hallie. Is that you? You sound out of breath."

Hallie closed her eyes and made a valiant effort to keep annoyance out of her tone. Brenda Fortune wasn't high on her list of people she enjoyed talking to. "Yes, mom. It's me. How are you?"

"Fed up," Brenda complained.

Uh-oh, Hallie thought. One of those calls. Ever the peacemaker, she asked softly, "What's wrong, Mom?"

"What's *not* wrong? That father of yours forgot to send my alimony check again. The court papers say he has to do it, but does he pay any attention? No, sir. He's probably spent every dime he's earned *and* my monthly check on that bimbo he's taken up with."

"Mom, Chelsa's not a bimbo." Close to it, but no sense adding fuel to the fire.

"How can you say that?" Brenda demanded. "She's only a few years older than you are."

So much for not adding fuel to the fire. Still, the reference was a little strong. "That doesn't make her a bimbo."

Brenda ignored Hallie's attempt to placate. "I give the man the best years of my life and look how it turned out. I swear, Hallie, if you ever meet a man who turns you on to the point you feel wrung inside out, run as fast and as far as you can."

Hallie battled with the discomfort of her mother discussing a turned on, sexual state and tried to push the image of Cody out of her mind. He definitely wrung her inside out. His touch was incendiary and immediate.

"Hallie? Did you hear me?"

"Yes, Mom. I promise I'll run." And she had been. "As to Dad, I'm sure you'll get your check soon. Dad understands his obligations."

"A fat lot you know. And why are you always taking his side of things anyway?"

"I'm not!" She just couldn't win where her parents were concerned. "I'm trying to make you feel better, Mom, and it's just not working. It never has. Do you remember when I was a little girl and I tried to convince you to leave? You didn't listen to me then. Why should you pay attention now?''

"There's no need to get snappy. I stayed for you."

I wish you hadn't. The words remained a mere echo in her mind. Hallie felt as if a vice had gripped her chest. She hated this constant dissension. Her parents were divorced, but they were still at it. And still putting her in the middle.

Hadn't she been a good girl? She'd done her best, but it never seemed to help. The fighting just went on and on. New day, new subject. From the color of the toast to the charges on the Visa card.

She took a deep breath, wishing she had the nerve to press the disconnect button. But that wouldn't be the good-girl thing to do, would it? she asked herself. "I'm sorry, Mom."

"I know, honey." Placated by the rote apology, Brenda's voice turned motherly. "It's hard to understand a relationship like your father's and mine. When it was good, it was *so* good, but that was usually in the bedroom."

Hallie was sure she didn't want to be discussing her parents' sex life. "Take heart, Mom. Now he's Chelsa's problem."

"And she's welcome to him—as long as he keeps sending my checks." Brenda paused. "Of course, he'll use her up soon enough and start playing around again. The man doesn't have a faithful bone in his body."

"What?" Hallie asked, stunned. She heard the bitterness in her mother's voice, but had trouble comprehending the words, even though they were plainly spoken. "Are you saying Dad had affairs?"

"You didn't know?"

"No." Hallie felt something inside her shatter. Something that felt close to failure. She didn't want to believe that all her efforts to keep peace in the family were in vain.

"I'm sorry, honey. I thought… Oh, it's just as well that you know. Learn from my mistakes, Hallie. Don't repeat them."

No, Hallie thought, feeling the band of sadness close around her chest like a pressure cuff inflated too tightly. She would not repeat her parents' mistakes, would not let passion rule her judgment.

HE KNEW SHE WAS THERE, under the oak tree. Rarely did he pass the lake, or that tree, without thinking of Hallie. Déjà vu slammed into him. Her sadness drew him. He told himself to let it go, to let her work it out on her own. He didn't deal well with problems, or sadness, never knew the right words to say. But Hallie Fortune was hard to resist. He hadn't been able to resist her as a kid. As a woman, it was damned near impossible.

"Seems like old times, huh?" he asked softly, easing down beside her on the grass-covered bank.

Hallie glanced at him, her wide brown eyes startled. "Where's Amy?"

"Hazel and George are fighting over her. Amy's loving it. Today's topic has something to do with gophers and firing a weapon in the city limits. I think they're keeping it up just to entertain her."

Hallie smiled, yet the spark in her expressive eyes was missing. He wanted to reach out to her, but didn't know how.

"How'd you know I was here?" she asked.

"I've always known when you were here."

Her eyes darted to his, surprised, skeptical.

He nodded. "I watched you." As a rebel teen, he wouldn't have admitted that. As a man, he had to. Hallie needed to know she wasn't alone—then and now.

"I never knew. Half the time you treated me like a pest."

"Because you scared me. Every time I looked into those big brown eyes I wanted to do things with you that would have shocked your good-girl sensibilities. I'm still having the same problem."

"Don't, Cody." She felt the weight of his stare, felt the gentle brush of his fingertips against her hair. Eye to eye they needed no words. What she saw in his gaze were the same emotions burning inside her.

It would be so easy to lean into him, to accept what his eyes offered. Her heart and body yearned for him, but her head said, *No way.* If he touched her he'd know how crazy she was for him, he'd feel it in her kiss.

Once she might have taken the risk. Now, she couldn't.

She looked out over the serenity of the lake's surface, feeling loneliness swoop down on her like a winter fog.

"You abandoned me, Cody."

"What?"

Hallie felt as startled as Cody sounded. She hadn't known the words were there. She hadn't known the *feelings* were there, yet they tumbled out, the feelings of a fifteen-year-old girl with a heavy case of hero worship.

"I needed you. You were my stabilizer, the one who kept me going when the fights got bad. I'd hope and pray you'd show up and somehow you would." Like fate.

Like the prediction of a fortune-teller. A prediction she'd foolishly taken literally—and had since learned to put into perspective.

"When you kissed me that day, you rocked my world and left me wanting. At fifteen, I didn't know what to do with that wanting. I was a good girl and suddenly I wanted to be bad. And then you were gone. You left me, Cody."

"I had to go, Hallie. The Marines were waiting."

"But you never told me you'd enlisted," she accused. "You didn't tell me you weren't coming back. I waited for you. Wished for you. I wanted to ask about you, but I couldn't."

"Why not?"

"Because then the hope would start all over again." Her gaze became unfocused. The faint smell of lush vegetation drifted off the lake as a soft summer breeze rustled leaves on the trees.

"My childhood dreams were built here at this lake," she said, her voice barely above a whisper. "And they were crushed here."

She didn't quite know why she was admitting this to him. Maybe it was this spot, this tree. Perhaps there was a mystical pull that encouraged openness, allowed for the telling of one's deepest secrets and desires. She and Cody had shared such times in the past, always after one of her parents' upsets. Perhaps it was inevitable.

He sat quietly, waiting, just listening. As a teen, Cody had been a guy of few words. He'd kept his secrets behind a tough barrier. Hallie had never had his restraint. With Cody, at the lake, her hurts had poured out like a pitcher overfilled. Like they did now.

"This used to be the place I ran to whenever I needed a friend. So many times I wished that you were here with me, as my friend." *And more.* "When you left I saw your face everywhere. It was hard on me."

"Wasn't there ever anyone else?"

Her gaze settled on him for a brief instant, then skittered away. With one strong arm propped on his bent knee, he was the picture of virility, her secret fantasy. A forbidden fantasy. He'd never known how deep her feelings for him ran. That was the one thing she'd managed to hold back from him. She didn't quite know why she was admitting to her girlhood crush now. Perhaps because as a woman she knew she wouldn't allow herself to be put in a position of rejection.

"I was involved with someone in college. A big mistake." A guy who'd been the recipient of all the aching hormones Cody had awakened in her. Her attempt at rebellion. Her one, disastrous walk on the wild side.

"Did *I* crush your dreams, Hallie?"

Her expression gentled. His deep voice was rich and smooth and soft with concern. The kind of voice that would draw millions on radio or TV. The kind of voice that drew a woman in, made her hang on every word, dream about that voice, that tone being focused on her, uttering words of passion...

Hallie blinked and shook herself out of the flight of fancy. Dear God, she was losing it. Big time. There was a time when she would have been foolish enough to fall for Cody, to believe in dreams and happily-ever-afters with a guy like him. That time was when she was a kid. Since then, she'd been burned by a bad boy, a volatile passionate bad boy who'd used her but refused to commit, who used anger and ugly words when she pushed too hard or got too close.

Cody had never used ugly words with her, but he fit the rest of the bill. He offered a passion that would burn too hot. And she just couldn't trust his staying power.

An echo of her mother's words came back to her. *If a man wrings your emotions inside out, run as fast and as far as possible.*

Through adult eyes, she understood what had happened with her parents. They'd entered into a marriage based on passion. And when the passion burned itself out, there was nothing left but the volatile emotions that had no outlet.

And that's what Cody aroused in her. Hot, immediate passion. An emotion she couldn't count on. Because the impressions of her childhood went too deep, the fears too high.

She'd set her course now. She had a date with Brian tonight. But the scorecard tally was leaning heaviest toward Tim.

Cody wasn't in the running. He broke all the rules of what she found acceptable—what was acceptable for her own peace…her heart.

Her head knew that. Convincing her heart would take a little doing.

She'd spent a lifetime searching for peace. The prediction of a fortune-teller had permeated her subconscious, an echo of hope. Rationally she'd dismissed the prediction, especially after Cody had left. Then rationally she'd examined it, given it more weight, spun dreams around it. The boy next door *type*. A safe guy. A man she could grow to love. Slowly. Peacefully. No lightning bolts.

"You didn't crush my dreams, Cody. Because those dreams were unrealistic. They were the dreams of a young girl who imagined what hope would feel like if it had a place in a lover's heart. I wasn't your woman, or your best girl, or even your friend, really, but you gave me something to remember. You said, 'always rely on yourself, Hallie. If you set your stakes too high on others you're bound to lose.'" And now she *was* relying on herself. On her scorecard.

"That was fifteen years ago. You were just a girl. You're a woman now. And I'm a man. Our playing field has different rules." Those kisses between them, especially the one two days ago, had made her skittish.

She looked at him, a sadness so crushing in her brown eyes it felt like a physical blow. "We weren't meant to be, Cody. At least not in this lifetime."

"I think you're wrong." If he hadn't crushed her dreams then there was hope. She responded to him. Passionately. But that passion scared her. A fear that went deep and covered many years, years of watching passion destroy a family. He wondered if he could get around her fears and knew that he had to try.

Because Hallie Fortune had become very important to him.

But she shook her head, denying him. Denying herself. He felt as if he were slamming up against a brick wall. He hadn't realized the powerful repercussions of kissing a fifteen-year-old Hallie. He'd taken something for himself that day, needing a taste, a remembrance to carry with him, never realizing she'd view his leaving as abandonment, never realizing what he'd done to her.

When will you stop walking away from your messes, Cody? Start taking responsibility? Miranda Brock's words echoed in his mind. He'd come a long way since that accusation.

He hadn't realized that Hallie was a mess he'd

walked away from. Hadn't known there was a need to atone.

Unwittingly, he'd contributed to the barriers she'd erected. She didn't trust him with her heart. He'd have to do something to change that. George Delong's words came back to him. The more he weighed the idea, the more he liked it.

"What you need is a case of good ol'-fashioned courting."

A bubble of laughter welled up and escaped before Hallie could call it back.

"You find the idea of me courting you funny?"

"Yes."

"I did say you had a knack for stepping on my ego."

"Cody." She sighed, wanting to succumb to his charm, yet knowing she couldn't. "Forget the courting stuff, okay? Just be my friend."

"Harlan and Darby are pals, Slick. I don't see us that way."

Her pulse leapt to a cadence of deep, powerful thuds. The sensual threat in his voice thrilled her, made her ache in ways she didn't know she could ache. She could smell the clean scent of his skin, see the dark stubble just beneath the surface on his strong jaw. Her heart pounded harder as he leaned closer.

The image of his lips caressing hers flashed across her mind. She couldn't do this! She was dating someone else. Well, two someone elses—as Cody had so diplomatically pointed out to her—but still, she owed them a certain amount of loyalty. At least until she figured out which of them would suit her needs for the future.

She shifted back from Cody and stood, brushing at the seat of her shorts. She saw his eyes narrow, saw the gentle amusement that flared in their blue depths.

The urge to reach out and trace the slight dimple in his strong cheek nearly undid her. She curled her fingers into her palms.

"Chicken," he taunted softly.

She made a clucking sound, grinned and held out a hand to him. "It's friends or nothing at all, Cody."

He gripped her hand and used her as leverage to hoist himself to his feet. The momentum brought her up against his hard body. From knees to chest they touched. Head bent, he stared at her.

Hallie held her breath.

A part of her wanted him to ignore her wishes, to act on the desire she saw so clearly on his features, a desire she was sure shone from her own. She wanted him to sweep her up and take her on a journey free of guilt, free of consequences, just one taste of the forbidden, a taste that she could savor for just a while.

Just one time. A quick, sultry walk on the wild side, a walk that would satisfy the craving once and for all.

But Hallie feared that one taste would never be enough. The craving would become an obsession. And life as she'd planned it would never be the same. The fate foretold by Sabrina now colored her thoughts, the direction she intended to travel. She didn't need to rely on silly hocus-pocus to know that she was terribly afraid there would be serious consequences if she messed with destiny.

She saw his head lower slightly. Although her heart screamed yes, her mind screamed no. She placed her fingers against his lips, her eyes begging him to understand, even though she knew she was sending him mixed messages.

"Friends, Cody?" Her voice trembled.

Strong, blunt fingers gently pushed the bangs from her temple. For an instant his palm cupped her cheek, and all the while, his intense blue eyes studied her. "I'll walk you back to the house…buddy."

He hadn't actually agreed to her terms, but it was close enough. Hallie didn't understand why she felt so bereft.

CODY SETTLED AMY on his hip and picked up the phone. Hazel Crowley's scratchy voice came over the line.

"You know she's got a date tonight, don't you?"

"Excuse me?"

"No need for that, boy. Brian Hollister's taking her to dinner at seven o'clock. He's a nice enough young man. Accountant. Something about him bothers me, though."

"What do you want me to do about it?" Hallie hadn't given him much encouragement that afternoon.

"You're a smart boy. You come up with something," Hazel suggested. "I'm just the meddling messenger." She cackled. "Actually, I won the toss. Beat George Delong out. He'll be grouching for a week."

She laughed again. "George wanted to do the calling. He said you were courting our Hallie."

Courting Hallie. He nearly snorted. He'd tried to suggest just that this afternoon and the little spitfire had laughed at him.

"Well," Hazel demanded. "Are you?"

Ah, hell. He'd always had a hard head. And more determination than was good for him at times. "If the lady will cooperate, I'll give it my best shot."

He hung up the phone and glanced down at Amy. "What do you say, squirt? Want to try our hand at messing up Hallie's date?"

Amy grinned, and raised her hands, babbling something he had no hope of understanding.

He answered as though she made perfect sense. He'd gotten pretty adept at that. "Exactly," he said, pressing his lips against her soft cheek. He snagged a diaper on his way to the bedroom. "Better get you changed and presentable. We've got a couple of things to do before Hallie's date shows up. There are rules to this courting stuff, you know. Slick's got a stubborn streak a mile wide, but we ought to be able to get around it."

"Sick," Amy repeated.

Cody glanced at his daughter, brow raised. She'd been trying to say "Slick." And her untutored speech pattern had just given him a hell of an idea.

He raised her high above his head, earning a delighted shriek. "Thank you, baby."

Chapter Seven

Brian had hardly gotten in the house before the doorbell rang. Apologizing to him, Hallie opened the front
door for the second time in a matter of minutes and
froze.

Cody and Amy stood on her porch.

He stared, as if he'd never seen a woman in a dress
before. She flushed with both embarrassment and
pleasure and tried to control the tremble in her hand,
tried to control the impulse to wipe her damp palm
against the gauzy fabric of her sundress. Tried to order her heart to settle down. None of her attempts
worked.

"Hallie?" Brian's voice directly behind her sev-
ered the electric current like the throw of a circuit
breaker. She backed up a step, keeping her hand on
the open door, about to gently tell Cody she was busy.

"Brian and I were just on our—"

"These are for you," Cody interrupted.

Sunflowers. She gripped the long stems he thrust
into her hands, feeling misty and hating it. Darn him.
Flowers would melt her anytime.

He took advantage of her lowered guard and waltzed right in, without invitation, arranging both Amy and the diaper bag as he slumped onto the couch.

Hallie's gaze darted to Brian, then back to Cody.

"Uh…Cody—"

"Brian, right?" Cody asked, his full attention centered on the man quietly simmering at her side. "We met the other day."

"The grocery store," Brian acknowledged tightly.

"Yeah. Sorry you couldn't join us. The steaks were okay. Would have been better if they'd had a touch more marble in them."

"I tried to point that out," Brian responded, obviously forgetting his head for the moment. He caught himself and frowned. Apparently he'd just remembered he hadn't intended to extend Cody an ounce of cordiality.

Cody grinned.

Hallie gaped at both of them and snapped her jaw shut. What a mess. A mess that promised to get stickier if she didn't put a stop to it.

She moved a step closer to Brian's side, irritated when his shoulders went back like some damned preening peacock. His jaw thrust forward rigidly. Sidetracked by the hostility radiating from him, she stared. He had no chin. Well, he did, but not much of one. Why hadn't she ever noticed that before?

"Sorry I took up so much of Hallie's time in the store," Cody said, not sounding sorry at all. "I'm a little new at this baby stuff. Hallie was a pal to help me out.''

When he said the word *pal,* his eyes darted to Hallie's. His meaning was more than clear and had nothing at all to do with buddies. She began to simmer. What kind of a game was he playing?

"No problem," Brian said, his shoulders relaxing. Hallie didn't know which one of them she wanted to hit the worst. Or first. Cody for taunting, or Brian for not recognizing when he was being had.

"Brian and I were just on our way out to dinner," Hallie said tightly, her brow arched at Cody.

"Oh. Sorry. I didn't mean to intrude." He glanced at Brian again, and darn it all, this time Cody truly did look apologetic. "It's this baby stuff again. I think she's sick."

Hallie's irritation vanished in an instant. Compassion flared and her nurse's antenna shot up. "What's wrong?"

"I'm not sure." Cody's palm covered Amy's forehead. The little girl rested in his lap quietly, her solemn, unblinking stare trained on Brian as if she expected him to pounce. She was normally timid around strangers. Then again, maybe she really was sick. That would account for the listlessness.

"I think she has a fever."

Hallie automatically reached for Amy's forehead, gauging its warmth. Her fingers got tangled with Cody's. Rather than doing the polite thing and giving her room, he turned his palm, linking their fingers together. Their gazes met over the top of Amy's head.

With her back to Brian, the other man couldn't see the contact, nor the fire that arced between them. Her hair fell forward, brushing his forearm.

"Damn you, Cody Brock," she whispered.

"How come you never wear your hair down for me?" he asked just as quietly.

Hallie all but hissed and jerked back.

Her eyes narrowed at the slow grin that crossed his face. It's a wonder she had any teeth left the way they were grinding. With as much calm as she could muster—given the fact that her insides were humming—she reached for her purse on the end table and slipped the strap over her shoulder.

"I think she'll be fine, Cody. It's probably just a low-grade fever from teething."

"So you *do* think she feels warm?"

Hallie shrugged, not liking the gleam in Cody's eye. "It could be from your own hand resting at her forehead."

"Did my hands feel warm, Slick?"

She ignored the bait. "Brian and I really have to go."

"Yes," Brian seconded.

"You're going to leave me with a sick baby on my hands?"

Enough was enough, already. He'd snagged her with the flowers. That was a low blow. She wouldn't allow him to play on her compassion. "Get a grip, Cody," she said testily.

He raised his brow at her tone. Amy frowned and gave a tiny whimper. Hallie felt like a monster. This wasn't like her. But, damn it. She had plans. And those plans didn't include Cody. She wasn't altogether certain about Brian's suitability. She'd begun to have serious reservations based on his actions of late. But she'd vowed to give him one last chance, to see how quickly he snapped out of his moodiness. That chance was tonight. At dinner.

And Cody was doing his level best to keep her from it.

She gave Amy a smile by way of apology and lifted the child's tiny hand for a quick kiss.

"I really need to get going, Cody," she said softly.

"Do you?" His raspy whisper carried no farther than her ears.

She nodded and he stood, slinging the strap of the diaper bag over his shoulder, his little daughter held securely on one strong forearm. "He's not the one, you know."

"I'll be the judge of that."

"If you were *my* lady, I wouldn't be standing ten feet away, letting another man undress you with his eyes."

"Another man wouldn't dare." Oh, no. She'd just admitted that Brian didn't measure up to Cody. And being a sharp guy, Cody hadn't missed the admission, or its meaning.

"Have a good time, Slick."

Aggravated at her slip, Hallie thrust out her chin. "I intend to."

"And don't worry about us," he tossed out just

before he stepped through the door. "If the baby gets bad, I'll dial 9-1-1."

Hallie rolled her eyes. She'd never thought to see such drama coming from bad-boy Cody Brock.

"IS THE FOOD not to your liking?"

"No, it's fine." Hallie pushed the breaded fish around on her plate. It was one of the café's specials. Ever the thrifty accountant, Brian had subtly suggested those choices. "It's this darn heat wave we're having. My appetite vanishes when the humidity rises. Who would think it would get this hot with only a few days before the end of summer." The fruit plate served with sherbet had looked better, but it had cost three dollars more. She should have ordered it and paid the difference.

"The weather service said we might get some rain by the end of the week. The rain should put an end to the heat spell."

Hallie was sure she'd never had this much trouble finding conversation topics with Brian. Had she? Pretty bad when all you could think to talk about was the weather.

And it was all Cody's fault, she decided. She couldn't concentrate. She should have been rating Brian's assets. Instead, all she could think about was Cody's sizzling blue eyes.

And Amy's drooping eyelids.

"Oh, no. They *were* drooping."

"Excuse me?" Brian quickly looked down at his

shirt front, then at hers, his nondescript hazel gaze lingering on her breasts. "What's drooping?"

She put down her fork and rested her elbow on the Formica table, unobtrusively blocking her breasts from his view. "Amy's eyelids. And she was listless. Didn't you notice that she was listless?" She didn't give him time to answer. "I should have taken her temperature."

"But you did."

"Not with a thermometer. I only felt her."

"Hallie, you're a nurse. If the kid had a bad fever, you'd feel it without the benefit of a device."

"No. That's not always so. Cody's hand had been covering her forehead. I passed it off as the warmth from his body, but I could have been wrong."

"Hallie, do we have to talk about Cody Brock? I'd thought to use this time to discuss us."

That prospect sent a cold shiver up Hallie's spine. "I wasn't talking about Cody. I'm worried about his daughter."

"Either way, it boils down to him. You should be careful around that guy."

"Why?" Her tone turned unfriendly.

"Why? The guy's been in jail, for God's sake."

"Do you know that for a fact?" Hallie asked carefully, so carefully her teeth ground together.

"Aunt Lucinda said—"

She didn't let him finish. "Your Aunt Lucinda was passing along gossip. I'm surprised at you for listening, and for attempting to repeat it."

"The gossip wasn't aimed at you, Hallie. But it could be if you don't watch your step."

"What?" Several months ago, she'd mentioned to Brian how gossip had hurt her as a child. She couldn't believe he'd more or less toss that in her face. Aside from her own feelings, though, she was more affronted on Cody's behalf. "It doesn't matter who's being talked about. Words can hurt."

"Since when did you become an expert on your jailbird neighbor?"

Hallie very carefully placed her napkin beside her plate. She avoided scenes at all costs. And this conversation looked as though it could very well turn into one.

"Brian, I think we should drop the subject."

"You're the one who brought it up."

"Well excuse me all to hell for being worried over a sick child. You've got the compassion of a gnat, Brian Hollister." Her voice raised, drawing stares from the other diners.

Mortified, angry and liberated...yes, liberated, damn it, she tossed her fork on to her plate. It made a satisfying clatter and sprayed cold peas clear across the table into Brian's lap. With trembling hands, she rooted through her purse and slapped several bills in front of her so-called date.

"Here's my share for the meal. That should satisfy your accountant's sense for checks and balance. We're even."

"For God's sake, Hallie. Lower your voice. People are staring."

Yes, they were. She'd never done anything so bold in her life. Acting on pure adrenaline, she hoisted her purse to her shoulder. "Let's cut our losses right here and now, why don't we? This relationship isn't going anywhere and there's no sense pretending otherwise."

"Hallie!"

"Don't bother to get up. I'll enjoy the walk home."

"I'll drive you."

"Why? You were happy enough to leave me in the grocery store. And that's farther away than this café. Enjoy your special, Brian." She glanced down at his plate of watery spaghetti. "And your life."

IT TOOK THE ENTIRE walk home for Hallie's temper to cool down. The heat didn't help. She'd never acted that way in her life. Might as well blame Cody for that, too. He tapped into her passion, made her want to test that wild streak she'd spent a lifetime suppressing.

Well, no more. As good as it had felt to tell Brian off, she couldn't handle a steady diet of these emotions. It took too much out of her. She needed peace.

She wouldn't find that peace with Brian. Hell, his points were farther in the negative than Cody's. Fool me once, shame on you, she thought. Fool me twice and I'm the idiot. How could her judgment have been so wrong?

She'd thought she'd wanted to rein in her temper. The closer she got to home, the more she realized she didn't want to. Cody Brock was through messing with her life, with her emotions and with her dates!

She'd worked up a good head of steam by the time she knocked on Cody's door.

And almost lost that steam when he answered the summons.

He didn't have a shirt on, damn him.

"You're home early, Slick. I didn't hear a car."

She shoved him out of her way and stomped into the room. "I walked."

"You what?" His voice had gone deadly quiet.

"Don't get that macho fighting stance. It was my choice."

"Explain."

"I don't owe you any explanations." Temper boiling, she glared at him. "You set me up, Cody."

One of his dark brows raised.

"Well?" she demanded when he just stood there.

"Well, what? You just said you don't owe me explanations, so I'm not asking."

"Oh, that's just like you. Turn it around on me."

"I'm lost, Slick."

To be honest, so was she—she'd lost the thread of the conversation, anyway. Staring at his bare chest and broad shoulders, she simply couldn't remember her point. She saw his tattoo clearly now, riding the rise of the muscle on his upper arm—hands clasped in friendship with a word below it that she couldn't make out from this distance.

He ambled over to the reclining chair, sat and picked up a beer, saluting her. "There's more in the fridge. Help yourself."

"You're drinking?"

"I'm having a beer, yes. Last time I checked, though, I didn't have a buzz."

"But you're combative. I can see it in your expression."

"Who wouldn't be? It's demoralizing to sit by and watch a lady you've got the hots for go on a date with another guy."

"That's crass, Cody." Blood rushed to her head and her heart stumbled.

"What? That I have the hots for you? I've never been good at pretty flowery words."

"Bull." The uncharacteristic word earned her a raised brow. He did just fine with words. "What happened to our agreement to be friends?"

He shrugged, staring moodily at his beer can. "I don't remember an agreement. So what happened with boy-o Brian?"

"Nothing." She wasn't about to tell him she'd caused a scene in the middle of a busy café—defending *him*. "Amy wasn't sick, was she?"

"I was right about him, wasn't I? Did you notice his weak chin?"

"Yes, I noticed. And that's beside the point."

"His chin?"

"Don't confuse me, Cody. Why did you lie about Amy?"

"Who says I lied?"

"You mean she's really sick? Where is she?" She automatically headed for the bedroom.

His feet came off the ottoman with a thud. "For

God's sake, Slick. Don't wake her up. I'll never get her back down.''

"I won't wake her. I'll just look."

Moodily, he watched how the gauzy dress moved with her slender body, floating around her in femininity. The smell of lavender filled his house and his senses, Hallie's scent. He hated that another man had spent the evening in her company, drinking in her serene features, imagining what his fingers would feel like running through all that unbound platinum hair, absorbing her scent and her essence.

He wanted to know why she'd walked home, what kind of an idiot would *let* a woman walk home after dark. Perhaps he'd go check out the guy's accounting fees and get a few things straight in the process.

He got up to get another beer. The look on Hallie's face when she saw the full can made him pause.

"Don't start, Hallie. I'm not drunk."

"Maybe not. But alcohol can alter your judgment. You might not react quick enough to Amy's needs if something were to happen."

"Did you stop by just to predict gloom and doom? I've had a full, frustrating day. I don't intend to get drunk. Just unwind." He'd learned his lesson about drinking to excess.

"That's what my parents used to say," she murmured.

He'd forgotten. She wasn't judging him so much as reacting to the consequences alcohol had had in her household. "Want me to pour it out?"

"No." What she'd really like was for him to put

on a shirt. "I'm just being silly. I'm probably still reacting to that phone call from my mom this morning. Unlike you, I didn't have perfect parents."

Hallie realized she'd said something wrong by the stiffening of Cody's shoulders.

"What do you know of my life, Hallie? Our folks didn't socialize with one another. After I left, did you become bosom buddies with Miranda and Gerald?"

Miranda and Gerald? Why did he call them by their first names? And why did she detect a spark of jealousy in his question?

"No. Your folks and I were only passing acquaintances. With my parents' reputation for fighting, we weren't exactly on the neighborhood list for backyard barbecue invitations. Besides, after you left, your parents bought the motor home and started traveling."

She was instantly sorry she'd mentioned the motor home. They'd been killed in an accident in it. The veins in Cody's forearm stood out as his grip tightened on the beer can.

"Grandparents," he muttered moodily.

Hallie frowned. "Who?"

"Gerald and Miranda Brock were my grandparents. My mother's alive and well...someplace."

Her jaw went slack. The man *was* drunk. Or delusional.

Chapter Eight

"Don't look at me like I've lost my mind, Slick. My grandparents adopted me."

Suddenly she recalled Edna Fitzpatrick referring to Amy as Miranda's *great*-grandbaby. The woman hadn't been confused after all. Cody's *sister* was his biological mother. "I never knew."

"Neither did I until I was fourteen. Did you ever meet Tamera?"

Hallie shook her head. "I knew *of* her, and that she was quite a bit older than you. But I never met her."

"No great loss," Cody said. "During one of her brief visits she happened to get in a fight with Mom— Miranda," he corrected himself.

"Cody, don't." Hallie reached out to him. Touching in compassion came second nature to her. "Miranda raised you. That earns her the title of Mom."

"Yeah." His head fell back against the recliner. "It's too bad it took me so long to figure that out. Anyway, Tamera got into it with Mom and dropped the bombshell that I was actually hers. Something like that has a way of sucking the foundation right out from under you.''

''And that's why you acted out the way you did.''

''Probably. For a while, I wanted to punish everyone in the household. They all lied to me. And my own mother abandoned me. There wasn't any good reason that I could see for her to blurt out the truth the way she did. It wasn't as if she was all set to take me off with her, or to move back in and try to be a parent. She was out of here that same day.''

''Have the two of you talked about it?''

''Tamera and I have a cordial truce between us. She doesn't have maternal instincts and doesn't apologize for it. It's easier to just think of her as my sister.'' He sipped his beer. ''So you see, that perfect family you apparently envied wasn't so perfect after all.''

''Did you…'' She didn't quite know how to ask her question. ''Did you make peace with them before…''

His Adam's apple worked on a deep swallow. ''The last thing I said before they left California—the day before I went to Desert Storm—was that I loved them.''

Hallie's throat ached with unshed tears. This conversation was tough on him. His memories were tough on him. She had an idea he'd given himself much more grief over the past than was warranted.

''They died on their way home from California. I was already over in Saudi by then. The authorities contacted Tamera. She made the decision not to no-tify me. I guess in her own way, she was afraid. She figured my grief might make me get sloppy over there and get myself blown to bits. I didn't find out about the accident for weeks. By the time I could get to a phone to call, I never got an answer. I told myself they'd decided to make a detour on the way home— they did that, just got in that damned motor home sometimes and went wherever it took them.''

He raked a hand through his hair. ''They should have traveled years sooner instead of being saddled with a rebellious grandkid to raise.''

''Cody, don't.''

''It's hard not to think that way, Slick. I took their golden years.''

''No. They chose to *give* you their best years.''

''Whatever. When they didn't answer my phone calls after another week, I called Tamera and got the news.'' He rubbed a hand over his bare chest as if his heart ached. ''I hate it that I didn't go to the funeral, that I didn't have any closure. That even now, six years later, I still don't have that closure.''

''Why didn't you come back sooner? The house has been empty for years.''

The beer can made wet circles on the end table as he pushed it back and forth. ''I drove by a couple of times when I got out of the service in 1995, but I couldn't bring myself to stop. So I rented an apartment in Chicago. The *Pals* strip had taken off by then and I could work anywhere.''

She hated to see Cody so tortured with memories and sought to ease the hurt. She noticed his storyboards strewn on a waist-high bench. It gave Hallie a thrill to see the actual drawings of the hood in a leather jacket and the nerd with a book in his hand. She'd been eagerly scouring the funny papers lately, looking for Cody's strip.

She moved over to his worktable, wanting to touch, yet resisting. "I'll bet they were proud of your cartoon strip."

"They never knew. I didn't want to say anything until I was sure it would fly. By then it was too late."

She'd meant to ease his hurt, subtly change the subject, but had blundered right back in. She tried once more. "How'd you get started in cartoons?"

"Dennis."

She glanced over her shoulder. She wished she knew what he was thinking. His gaze tracked her like a magnet, never wavering. "Dennis? As in Darby?"

Cody nodded. "I was always drawing stuff. The pictures started to evolve into mine and Dennis's experiences of the day. He'd razz me and I'd fire right back at him. Pretty soon, the cartoon characters had dialogue. Dennis knew the editor of the *Chicago Tribune* and he kept hounding me to send the drawings in. Finally I did. More to shut him up than anything."

She caught his scent before she actually realized he'd gotten up and moved behind her. The heat from his body surrounded her. Her fingers trembled against the edge of the table.

"They ran the strip and asked for more. Before I knew it, *Pals* was picked up by a syndicate."

Hallie cleared her throat and scooted closer to the

drawing board. From the corner of her eye she could see Cody's broad, shirtless shoulders. It took all her willpower not to turn and press against him, skin to skin, hips to hips, lips clinging in frenzy....

She sucked in a breath and took a step to the side, feeling crowded, terrified...thrilled. "Uh, do you still see Dennis?"

Although they weren't touching, she felt him stiffen, felt the emotions radiating from him. "Dennis died."

Hallie did turn then, laying her hands against his bare chest in comfort, ignoring the fire that scorched up her arms. "Oh, Cody, I'm so sorry."

"Yeah. Me, too." He placed his palm over the back of her hand, trapping her. She meant to pull away, but didn't. Everybody needed touch. Especially in times of grief, if only remembered grief.

"Do you...?" She shook her head. "Never mind."

"I can talk about him. I couldn't for a while. The strip has helped. Therapy in a way."

He stepped around her, leaning an elbow on the edge of the table, studying the Darby character. Close now, Hallie saw the word tattooed above the clasped hands. *SemperFi*. She wondered what it meant.

"After Desert Storm, Dennis went to Saint Thomas. Said that's where all the cute girls were. He'd planned to bum around for a while, be a bartender on a sandy beach somewhere. Then he started getting tired and losing weight. He tried to joke about not feeling up to speed, but he just wasn't his usual self. The more I thought about him, the more it bugged me. So I hopped a plane to Saint Thomas." His gaze raised to the ceiling.

"Man, Hallie, he was gone within hours after I got there."

Hallie's arms were around him before he even finished his sentence. She held him to her with a strength that surprised him. In silence he took from her, allowed her soft body to draw the sadness from his soul. He felt her heart pound against his chest, felt her warm breath against his shoulder. The clock over the mantel chimed ten o'clock. His own arms naturally slipped around her slender waist, his fingers tangling in the ends of her silky hair.

He knew the exact instant that comfort turned to desire. Her breathing changed almost imperceptibly, becoming shallow, strained. His arms tightened around her, his palm nearly spanning the width of her back. She felt so small, so right.

His lips caressed her ear, her cheek and at last her mouth. The scent of lavender wafted around him, heat scorched him. He tasted desire on her lips, and he tasted reserve.

He wanted her with a desperation that made him ache, and he knew he couldn't have her. If he kept kissing her, he knew he'd try to coax her into the bedroom. And despite her determination to press forward with this safe course she'd set for herself, her adamance to be just friends, he figured there was a damned good chance she'd let him.

His lips lingered for an agonizing moment more. It took every ounce of control he possessed to pull back, to meet her dazed brown eyes, eyes that were already turning wary, filling with regret.

He, too, felt that regret. Felt it deep inside him in a place that hurt like hell. She made him want things he'd never dreamed of wanting. Impossible things.

"Well," Hallie said, clearing her throat and straightening her dress. "That was…something."

"Yeah," he said softly. "Definitely something."

She didn't like the way he watched her so intently. It made her nervous. As if any minute now he'd pounce.

"That dress is driving me crazy," he said out of the blue, his gaze dropping to her chest. "Feminine. Flirty."

She knew better than to let him draw her in this way. Distance. That's what she needed.

She walked across the room with studied nonchalance and sank down on the sofa, the enormity of the evening's events weighing her down like a wet blanket. "I'm glad you like my dress."

"Did Brian?"

She remembered Brian's gaze centering on her chest. It had annoyed her, made her feel creepy. Cody had done the same thing, yet she hadn't felt affronted. In fact, she'd felt a little wild.

"Oh, Cody. I caused a scene at the café," she blurted.

"You?"

"I know. You're shocked. I am, too."

"What did you do?"

She told him, forgetting to leave out the jailbird part.

"You defended me?"

"Of course. I always defend my friends." She stressed the last word, hoping to steer them back on the right track. That kiss, like the others, was going to get in the way if she allowed it. "It wasn't fair of Brian to repeat gossip that way. *You* didn't know the car was stolen."

A dimple flashed in his cheek. "You believed me? Just like that?"

She didn't even hesitate. "Yes. You might have howled at the moon on Saturday nights or shot out the streetlights in town." A smile tugged at her lips. "You were never an angel, Cody. I saw you myself doing a good eighty miles an hour in the city limits on that motorcycle of yours. The one thing you never did, though, was lie to me."

"Thanks, Slick. That means something to me."

"Of course it does. It means we're friends."

"Does it?" His penetrating gaze held enough wattage to melt her on the spot, her vocal cords included.

Rather than try to speak, she nodded, suddenly uncertain of his mood, of his stillness. Desire palpitated in deep intangible waves, spinning a silky, mesmerizing web, holding her in its spell. Then Cody moved, as if the moment had never happened.

"I'd liked to have seen you in action. I bet it was something."

Shifting mental gears once again, Hallie grinned—

even though a part of her was appalled at her behavior at the café. "Brian wears cold peas well."

Cody laughed, his voice deep and rich. She wanted to just curl up and listen to him all night. She dismissed the thought.

"So, is he now officially off your list?"

"Yes, I can safely say he is."

"Okay. So that just leaves me and the banker."

Hallie's heart skipped a beat. "Tim, yes. *You* are not on the list."

"Yes, I am," he said softly, dangerously, challenging her to dispute it.

Good Lord, he *had* seen the page with his name on it. Warmth flooded her face. She pretended that it hadn't. "If you were on my list, you'd only appear in the Con column."

"I don't think so. I brought you flowers. You love flowers. Definitely a plus."

"Tim brings me flowers," she argued.

"Sunflowers?"

No. Never. "Flowers are flowers."

"Not to you."

Hallie glanced at the clock. "Would you look at the time. I've got to get home."

He stepped in front of her when she would have headed for the door. "Put me on your list, Slick. Let's see how I do against the other guy."

She shook her head. *Passion is at the root of your problem.* Sabrina's words flashed across her mind, raising the hair on her arms. If she didn't know better she'd swear the words had been said aloud. Spoken or not, the reminder was all it took to set her straight again. Cody's kisses could make her forget all reason. He could have invented passion. And that was all wrong for her. She had it on the authority of a fortune-teller, who was a wise woman, to boot. But she didn't need a clairvoyant to tell her, she had the memories of her parents' disastrous, passionate life to reflect back on.

And if by any chance her destiny meant repeating her parents' mistakes, she didn't want any part of it.

Before she did something really stupid, like allow herself to entertain Cody's suggestion, she smiled and gave his hand a brief squeeze.

"I value your friendship too much to mess it up. Besides, you've never given the impression that commitment's your thing."

"If you'd come to bed with me I could change your mind."

Warmth once again flooded her face. Hallie cursed the uncontrollable reaction. "Cody, you're talking about pure lust. You know how I feel about that."

"Yeah, and I think your measuring it by a lousy yardstick."

"I know my parents were lousy examples, but it's not very charming of you to point it out...*friend*."

"You're deliberately misunderstanding me."

"Probably."

He studied her long and hard, yet his thoughts and emotions were masked. "Okay. Have it your way... *friend*."

HALLIE CHANGED into a white satin chemise, loving the way the silky material slid over her skin. It made her feel sensual, sexy, dangerous.

The same way Cody made her feel.

Tonight she'd kept stressing the word *friend,* hoping to convince him when, actually, *she* was the one who needed the reminder. Cody made her want things she knew better than to want, made her act in ways she shouldn't. What in the world had gotten into her? And why was it becoming so hard to keep up the pretense she'd spent a lifetime cultivating so carefully?

She'd behaved badly in the restaurant with Brian, but she couldn't seem to work up much remorse. The show of temper had made her feel liberated, as if she'd just taken a vacation from herself.

The behavior was more suited to something Maggie would have done.

Needing to unwind, Hallie switched on the stereo. Music flowed from the compact disk, energizing and relaxing all at the same time. As the beat reverberated through her, she inched the volume up a notch, swaying to the sensual beat, feeling a freedom she usually didn't allow herself...feeling a little bit naughty.

Was this how Maggie felt when posing for a camera? Beautiful...reckless...naughty? Caught up in the emotion of the moment, she pictured herself as her cousin, imagined herself psyching herself up for the camera, playing to that lens, releasing her inhibitions, feeling beautiful, desirable, confident. For a brief few instants she actually became someone else, and it was

Cody's image she saw at the other end of the imaginary camera she played to, Cody's jarring blue eyes watching her, mesmerizing her.

In her imagination, she teased him, deliberately, luring him into her sensuality, spinning a spell so strong he was powerless to resist.

Her movements became more pronounced as his image filled her mind, her soul. Alone, with no one to witness the breech in her strict personal code, Hallie let herself dream, imagined that she was free to let loose the bad-girl streak she normally suppressed. Cody had done that to her; he'd slipped past her defenses, tapped into a yearning she knew she had no business entertaining.

But fantasies were safe. No one would ever know.

CODY FELT IRRITABLE...and restless. There was fire in the night, a moodiness that kept him from working.

He shoved his sketches aside and wandered into the kitchen. Fireflies flashed outside, blinking around the pear tree like haphazard strands of twinkling Christmas lights.

The frustration of wanting Hallie Fortune and not having her was beginning to mess with his mind. He'd taken more cold showers lately than he had in a long time. It hadn't helped—not with the September heat, nor the heat that burned deep inside him, caused solely by his stubborn, sexy, aggravating neighbor.

Friends. Hell. No way.

Resigned to try the shower again, he started to leave the kitchen. The faint sound of music held him in place. Something classical, light, sensual...sad in an eerie sort of way.

Coming from Hallie's house.

The breeze shifted, drawing the haunting strains his way, through the open window, filling his home, surrounding him. It wasn't the type of music he would have associated with Hallie. He hadn't imagined she'd play her stereo so loud, either.

Curious, he stepped out the back door, drawn by the sensual beat, drawn by a power he didn't understand. A strange mix of piano and organ, saxophone and drums. It created images of sadness one minute and lust the next. He'd never heard anything so beautiful, so powerful, so evocative.

The words sounded Latin but the emotional range of the vocalist transcended language barriers, telling a story. A story of slow, sensual touches, building in an erotic crescendo, a story of forbidden desires, of a sadness so deep it could draw tears from a stone. Soothing, yet urgent. A desperation made even more powerful by its forbidden nature.

Cody's heart pounded, his blood pumping through his veins, haunting him, creating madness.

Lights shone from Hallie's back windows. Through the partially open lace curtains of the sliding glass door, he saw her—swaying to the sensual beat.

He went utterly still, transfixed by the sight.

A lovers dance for one.

Louder now, the music called to him. And so did Hallie. He couldn't have looked away if his life had depended on it.

She was lost in the moment, in the heat. She had no idea he stood here, mesmerized, wanting, stunned and excited. A voyeur held prisoner by a desire so deep he ached.

The urge to join her nearly overpowered him. But he couldn't leave Amy. This was the worst kind of torture. So close, yet so far. Platinum hair framed her face like a halo, spilling down her back in a waterfall of silk. She wore a white filmy shift that skimmed her curves, held in place by spaghetti straps.

The rhythm carried her body in slow, sinuous movements, shoulders swaying, hips following with ease and grace as if she were boneless. Fluid movements that held him spellbound—so erotic in their simplicity.

She curved into the music, becoming one with it, making it impossible to tell where the harmony began and ended.

Images of dark sin clawed at Cody's insides, consumed him. He felt his soul drawn to her, to the music, as if he were right there in the room with her, touching her, easing up against her slender curves, moving with her.

Sweat dripped down his temples and pooled beneath his arms. His teeth gritted so hard his jaw cramped. Heart pounding, fists clenched, he closed his eyes and let his imagination fly, imagining the feel of silk beneath his palms, sliding her slip higher on her thighs, moving with her, slowly, softly.

The tribal beat of the music called to him. Pounding. Throbbing. Torturing. Reverberating through the walls of his chest...his soul.

His eyes sprang open when the music switched tracks. This beat was stronger, not as serene, evoking images of primal lust. The fire that burns so hot you think you'll die if you don't touch it.

His body felt coiled, primed to erupt in a dark, consuming madness.

And once again he was unable to look away.

Where before her movements had nearly hypnotized him, now they enticed beyond tolerance. Her body jerked and moved with the pulsating beat, faster, hotter, wilder, her long hair swinging, arms raised, reaching as if for a lover, a look of ecstasy on her features. He imagined a fine sheen of sweat coating her smooth skin, imagined tasting that sweet dampness, touching...

Damn it! This was too much.

He tried to move but couldn't. Something primitive held him in it's grip, something dangerous. He wanted to unleash that danger on Hallie in a way that would leave no room for any other man in her life. Wanted Hallie to behave this way with him, *for* him. But she wouldn't. Her fears went too deep, her normal reserve too strict.

Insides churning, he finally found the strength to turn away, to go back in the house before the last shred of his control snapped, before he succumbed to emotions that were screaming to be released, before he did something he knew Hallie wasn't ready for.

Sweet little Hallie Fortune.

Sexy-as-sin Hallie Fortune.

A woman he'd sell his soul to possess.

Damn, this woman had fire. No way in hell would the banker or the accountant be right for her.

Or any other man if Cody had anything to say about it.

Chapter Nine

Cody preferred not to work on Saturdays, but after Hallie's impromptu dance last night, he hadn't been in the right frame of mind to draw cartoons. At least none that weren't X-rated. So this morning he was playing catch-up.

"Daddy will be done in just a few minutes," he told his daughter who was holding on to the coffee table a few feet away, making a mess out of the magazines strewn on its surface. He'd gotten into the habit of keeping up an absent, running dialogue with his daughter, even while his hand flew furiously over the page, sketching characters by rote. The new characters, the baby and the nurse, were a stroke of genius in his opinion. The editor thought so, too.

From the corner of his eye, he could see Amy bobbing on unsteady legs as if dancing to her own private tune. At the sound of his voice, she babbled right back, only some of the words discernible. Her tiny voice got louder, indicating she was getting tired of being ignored.

He held out his left hand, palm up, his sketch pencil never pausing. "Okay. Okay. Almost finished."

When he felt tiny fingers grip his leg, his pencil skipped clear across the page. His head jerked.

Amy beamed up at him.

"Da Da."

It took a minute for Cody to find his voice. Then a grin split his face. "You walked! Oh, you smart baby."

He scooped her up and headed out the door. This kind of news had to be shared.

"Hey, Slick!" he hollered, mounting Hallie's porch steps in two strides. He pulled open the screen door and went in without stopping to think about politeness and manners. Hallie came out of the kitchen, drying her hands on a dish towel.

"Cody…?"

"She walked. One minute she was at the coffee table and the next she was holding my hand. Isn't she the smartest kid you've ever seen? Check it out."

He set Amy down on the floor. "Hold your hands out and see if she'll come to you. Walk, baby. Show Hallie what you did."

Hallie knelt and held out her hands as requested. Amy grinned and shrieked and toddled forward on shaky legs. The minute Cody's hand turned loose, though, Amy faltered.

In unison, they reached for the baby to break her fall, ending up in a gentle heap on the oriental rug decorated with cabbage roses. They stared at each other.

"Is this what you'd call a group hug?" Cody asked, the side of his mouth kicked up in a sexy grin.

"Something like that." Hallie started to pull away, but Cody's hands tightened over hers.

"Want to try again?"

She knew he was referring to Amy's first steps. His eyes, however, sent a different message. There was something charged and speculative in Cody's gaze, a warning that challenged her composure. It was as if he'd somehow tapped into the private fantasies she'd had last night. Which was ridiculous. She'd been alone.

He was still watching her, that sensual fire burning in his hot blue eyes. She cleared her throat and pulled her hand out of his hold. "Sure. If Amy's willing."

"Yeah. She's willing. Aren't you, kid?" He buried his lips in the baby's dark curls and chuckled. Like the flash of lightning, his expression cleared. It was as if the heavy sensuality had been imagined, confusing the heck out of Hallie.

"Look at you," he said to the baby. "What's that frown for? I didn't knock you down, you know. Lighten up, squirt." Encouraged by her fleeting grin, he tickled her tummy. Amy squealed and giggled. The giggle turned into a belly laugh, the laughter of an innocent child who was finally losing her reserve.

Hallie joined in the laughter. It was a sound no adult could resist.

"Hey," Cody said, sounding amazed. "She's happy. Just listen to those underused vocal cords sing!"

To see Cody react, a person would have thought Amy was the only baby on earth to ever laugh or take a first step.

"Okay. On your feet, squirt. Walk to Hallie. Don't make a liar out of your old man."

Once again, Hallie dutifully held out her hands and wiggled her fingers in invitation. This time, Amy managed three steps and tripped right into her waiting embrace. Hallie hugged and praised.

Cody sat back, watching his daughter, everything within him going soft at the obvious rapport Hallie had with the child. She'd make a great mother. Right now, he couldn't imagine not having either one of them in his life. He could do something to insure Amy's permanence. He wasn't so certain about Hallie, though. There was a reserve about her whenever he got too close. She kept stressing the word *friend*. He knew different. Last night's erotic dance continued to fill his mind. He considered telling her he'd watched, but decided to bide his time. Still, he wished for once she'd let her hair down like that for him.

One hurdle at a time, he cautioned himself.

"I need to find an attorney," he said.

Hallie looked up, easily positioning Amy so the little girl sat in her lap. "For what?"

"I want to make sure everything's legal...and permanent as far as Amy's concerned."

"You mean there's no custody agreement?"

"No. When Amy's grandparents called me, Tanya had already been gone for several months. They hadn't heard from her."

"She just abandoned her baby?" Hallie couldn't imagine anyone doing such a thing.

"That's the way I see it. The grandparents must have felt the same way. They were elderly, living on a fixed income that didn't stretch far enough to include a baby. When I got there, they handed me Amy's birth certificate naming me as the father and lab test results showing her blood type."

"So that's how you knew she was yours? Your blood types matched?"

"I didn't even check. I took one look at her and knew she was mine."

"It is pretty obvious. Still, for legal purposes, you might want to have a test done." She saw his jaw tighten and wondered about it. "Do you think Tanya will fight you if you sue for custody?"

"I don't see why she would, if I can even find her to begin with. She appears to be wrapped up in her own life and selfish needs. I've got some experience in that area."

"Your mother."

"My sister," he corrected. "I won't have Amy wondering where she came from. I'll tell her everything as soon as she's old enough to understand. But she needs stability. And I can give her that."

"Of course you can."

"And I'm learning all the right stuff. Look at her. Since she's been with me, she's happier. She laughs now, Hallie. She never laughed the first three weeks I had her."

Hallie's professional instincts perked up, giving her

a jolt of unease. "Cody, you don't think she was neglected, do you?"

"No. But Tanya's folks were older. The mom had arthritis and it was hard for her to lift Amy. I think they just sort of let her be, didn't talk to her much, teach her. I've been reading books about the stages of a child's development. You're supposed to show them stuff, raise them in stimulating surroundings with bright colors and movement and noise. I've been talking to her a lot, and she's starting to talk back."

"Cody, it's obvious you're doing a good job with her. You don't have to convince me."

"Yeah. But will I have to convince a court? A judge?"

Hallie shrugged. "They might assign someone to your case, maybe come out and look at your house. You've got a good job and you're a stay-at-home, Mr. Mom type. That should count heavily in your favor." Anyone with a set of eyes would never think to call Cody a Mr. Mom. Passionate bad boy, yes. Aprons and vacuum cleaners and car pools, no. "You don't have a police record, do you?"

"There's that image, again," he teased, yet beneath the teasing was an underlying thread of disappointment. "My record wasn't all that bad to begin with, but Mom had it sealed after I joined the Marines. I doubt there's any skeletons to come back and haunt me."

"Well, that's good. You know, I've got a friend who's an attorney. I'll give you his number if you like."

"Define *friend*."

The demand, as well as his tone, caught her off guard. "You're a friend."

"That's what I was afraid of." He sighed and ran a hand through his hair, hair that had begun to grow out and curl at his nape. "Tell me this guy's sixty years old."

"No. He's about thirty-five."

"Married?"

"No. Cody, why are you asking me these questions? If you don't like Derek, you can just as easily look in the phone book and come up with any number of attorneys who specialize in family law."

"I'm just trying to make sure it's law the guy specializes in and not you."

"Don't be ridiculous." Hallie set Amy on the floor and got to her feet. Derek *had* asked her out a few times. "Do you want his number or not?"

"Yeah." Cody scooped Amy up and followed Hallie into the kitchen. Pies rested on each burner of the stove. Two more cooled on sunflower pot holders on the countertop.

"I thought I smelled apple pie. Are you going to eat all of them or are you willing to share?"

"I'll share..." She glanced over her shoulder as she flipped open her address book. "...with the whole town. They're for the Founder's Day parade, so stop drooling."

"Amy drools. I don't."

"Excuse me. Not the macho thing to do, huh?"

"Well, under the right circumstances..."

She glanced at him sharply, knowing exactly where his thoughts had wandered. Her breasts tightened at the suggestion in his tone. "Don't start, Cody. It's too early in the morning."

He shrugged innocently. Too innocently. "I've always found mornings to be pretty good."

Hallie ducked her head, letting the strands of her hair shift around her face. She knew her cheeks had reddened and cursed the reflex. "Cody, you're a menace. Here's the number." She scribbled the digits on a piece of paper and handed it to him.

"Guess I'll just have to join in with the town if I want a piece of your pies, huh?"

"Guess you will."

"What do you say we go together?"

"I was about to leave when you showed up." Spending the day with Cody wasn't what she'd intended. She needed distance, needed to stop the fantasies. She needed safety and peace.

"That's fine. It'll only take a few minutes to grab Amy's stuff."

Hallie hedged. "I really should get these pies there."

"It's not like they'll spoil or anything. Do you have a date?"

"No. I'm meeting up with some friends."

"Perfect. You can introduce Amy and me around. Since this is our home, we might as well mingle with the locals, get involved. It'll look better to the judge, too."

"Did you plan this?" she asked suspiciously. "Your timing's incredible lately."

Cody grinned. "There isn't a devious bone in this body."

Hallie rolled her eyes.

"Besides, it's lucky for you that mine and Amy's timing's so perfect. You'll need help carrying all those pies."

"That's what the cardboard boxes are for."

"Come on, Slick. What are you afraid of?"

"I'm not afraid." *Liar.*

"Then give in and agree to ride with me. Amy and I were planning to go anyway. This way we'll have a friend to hang out with."

"Definitely devious," she said. Darn him for tossing the word *friend* in her face.

THE FIRST THING Cody did after loading the stroller, the pies, Amy and Hallie into the Blazer was to turn off the radio. He didn't need music to remind him of last night, didn't trust himself not to respond to the deep vibrations of bass coming from the stereo.

He was doing his damnedest to keep up the friend pretense Hallie insisted on holding him to. Watching her bend over in tight jeans as she adjusted Amy's car seat restraints made his good intentions go south. Her scent filled his car, teasing him, threatening his concentration.

"We probably could have walked," Hallie said.

"Yeah, but those clouds are looking like they mean

business. I'd hate to get caught in a downpour with the baby.''

Finding a parking spot was a little dicey. The whole town had turned out for the celebration. One hundred percent participation in community events was an unwritten law in small towns, a law the population had apparently taken to heart.

The parade had already started down Main Street. Mayor Williams rode in a '56 T-bird convertible, waving to his friends and neighbors. Behind him, Parkdale High School's band marched in formation.

''Good old orange and black,'' Cody commented, lifting the Blazer's hatchback to retrieve the pies. ''I always thought those were awful school colors.''

''Too Halloweenish for you?'' Hallie had already gotten Amy out and was expertly unfolding the stroller. ''If you'd played football like Coach wanted you to, you might have gained a little more pride in our colors.''

''Hey, I didn't have time for football.''

''Too busy under the bleachers with Jeanie Atkins?'' Hallie asked dryly.

''Jealous, Slick?''

''Not hardly.'' *Majorly.* ''We'll drop the pies off at the fire station. That's where all the food's supposed to be set up.''

The smell of charcoal fires permeated the air. Long tables laden with every potluck dish imaginable graced the drive of Parkdale's fire department.

''Smart thing to assign the firemen cooking duty,'' Cody noted.

"Yes. If the charcoal gets out of hand, they've got the equipment to deal with it. Wouldn't that be a sight, though. A fire hose on a barbecue pit."

"I heard that," Steve Moyer said, coming up behind Hallie and giving her a bear hug. "Picking on us again, Hal?"

It took everything Cody possessed and then some to keep from snatching the fireman's hands off of Hallie and decking the guy just for the pure pleasure of it.

"Fire hoses aren't the only equipment we've got. When are you gonna make my dreams come true and marry me?"

A hell of a lot of control, Cody thought, his hands tightening around the handle of the stroller.

"Why, Steve," Hallie teased. "Are you asking?"

"I've asked every time I've seen you, sweetheart."

Hallie laughed, a happy, throaty sound that held Cody spellbound. "And if I accepted, it'd scare you to death." She turned to Cody. "Steve, this is Cody Brock. Cody, Steve Moyer."

Steve held out a hand. "Nice to meet you. New in town?"

"Relatively."

"You'll like it here." The fireman reached down and tickled Amy's chin. "Good place to raise kids."

"You have kids?" Cody asked. He started to relax his choke hold on the stroller.

"Nope. I'm free as a bird and I like it that way."

Relief shot straight back to steel-bending tension. That's what he was afraid of.

"Uh, Steve?" Hallie said.

"Yeah?"

"You're burning those hamburgers."

The fireman whirled, spatula in hand and raced across the driveway, snatching up a squirt bottle on his way.

"These are firemen?" Cody asked rhetorically.

Hallie grinned. "Mmm. And they have a reputation for knowing how to cook. Scary, huh?"

They placed the pies on the table along with the other desserts, then moved out into the throng of parade watchers.

"So, how come old Steve's not on your scorecard."

"Cody, I wish you'd stop with the references to my list."

"Why? I have a personal stake in it."

"No, you don't."

"You mean you took me off?"

"You were never on it."

"I beg to differ." For an instant, sound receded. The look that arced between them left no room for celebrations or crowds or the clang of cymbals from the marching band. It was the type of look that required privacy and soft lights and sensual concentration.

His gaze dropped to her lips, then to the pulse he could see beating at her neck. He wanted to bundle her right back into the car and race home with her— straight to his bed.

Amy's delighted shriek at the sight of Clydesdale horses broke the spell.

"So, what's wrong with the fireman?" he asked, unable to drop the subject of her comparison chart.

Hallie blinked and swallowed, drawing a deep breath as she glanced around the crowd, obviously looking for witnesses to the charged moment. "He's a player."

"Ah." She might as well have said, *just like you.* Perhaps that reputation might have applied once, but he was a father now. He'd turned over a new leaf and, damn it, she should have noticed.

Children were lined up behind a streamer, their excited voices raised as they prepared to race their decorated bikes along a preset course. Even little tykes were included, their tricycles sporting streamers and plastic horns and bright colors. Amy leaned forward in her stroller, her busy eyes taking in everything at once.

Everybody who passed by spoke to Hallie. Those Cody didn't know were introduced. The ones he *did* know appeared to want a scaled-down version of the last fifteen years of his life.

The baby's name is Amy, he'd repeated so often it felt automatic. *She's eleven months old. Yes, she's small for her age. No, Amy's mom's not in the picture. Yes. I've been gone awhile—spent two hitches in the Marines. Yes, Desert Storm was tough. Yes, I plan to stay in Parkdale. Yes, I'm the Brock who draws* Pals. *No, the Kiwanians haven't approached me yet for membership.*

In small towns, it was almost impossible to keep to oneself. The old ladies were taken with Amy. The younger women were taken with him. It wasn't ego that made that observation. A few of them had been blatantly obvious. Hell, a curvy brunette had just brazenly slipped her phone number in the hip pocket of his jeans. Stunned, Cody whipped around, checking to see if Hallie had noticed.

She had.

"Damn it, Hallie," Cody complained as the woman walked away, glancing back over her shoulder. "How could you just stand there and let that woman stick her hands down my pants?"

She shrugged. "What did you want me to do?"

"Protect me."

"Come on. A tough-guy ex-Marine needing protection? From a *female?*"

"Look, I'm not in the market to increase my little black book. Be a buddy if that happens again and get physical, would you?"

"Physical like in scratching her eyes out?"

"You don't have to go that far. Put your arms around me, kiss me, stick to me like flypaper. Anything. Just don't let that happen again."

"You poor thing. It's tough being so sexy, isn't it."

"You think I'm sexy?"

"I'm not answering that. You're entirely too cocky as it is."

"I'm not cocky. I'm terrified. That woman put her hands in my *pants!*"

Hallie linked her arm through his and nudged the stroller forward. "Okay, pal. I'll protect you. But only to a point. I'm not giving the town a reason to gossip about our relationship. Tim's understanding, but there's no sense putting him in an awkward position."

"What about those dinners you had with the accountant? How'd he feel about that?"

"He wasn't threatened. Besides, I never kissed Brian."

"But you've kissed the suit?"

"Stop calling him the suit. And yes, I've kissed him."

"Let me guess. Nice and neat. Good technique. But when he's done, there isn't a hair on your head out of place. And not a spark of fire burning between you."

"Cody, I'm not discussing Tim's kisses with you!" Good grief, he'd described them down to a tee. At least Tim was predictable, though. Safe. Reliable. He wouldn't dream of threatening her with improper suggestions and she never had to wonder about his moods. Life with Tim would be easy. Good.

She couldn't say the same thing about life with Cody Brock.

"Where is the top scorer, by the way?"

He was referring to her scorecard again. Hallie had an urge to sock him. "He's out of town on business."

Cody's brows rose mockingly. "The bank manager missing Founder's Day?"

"It's an important convention." Change the subject, she told herself. "There's Derek Engle, the attorney I told you about," she said. "Why don't I go introduce you."

"Do you know every single man in town?"

"Probably."

The man Hallie introduced him to was well over six feet and close to Cody's own age. Assessing him man to man, Cody decided that women would find Derek Engle attractive. He didn't come on to Hallie in a flippant playboy style, but his squared shoulders and self-assured carriage made Cody uneasy. So did the banked fire burning behind the other man's sharp eyes.

Derek Engle looked at Hallie the way a man looks at a woman he wants. A woman he wants and intends to have. Cody recognized the look because he knew it was in his own eyes.

This was no Milquetoast fool who could be easily led. And that worried the hell out of Cody. This was a guy who could give him a run for his money.

"A custody dispute?" Derek asked after Hallie outlined Cody's problem.

"Not a dispute, yet," Cody said, making every effort to be civil. "I don't want any surprises, though."

"I hear you. If you want me to handle it for you, give my secretary a call on Monday and set up an appointment. It should be a fairly easy process, provided we can track down the mom. We'll go in on grounds of abandonment. I've got to tell you, though, I'm not cheap. If it turns out to be more involved, it could get expensive."

"Expense isn't an issue," Cody said, stating fact

rather than bragging, establishing his own worth and determination. Hallie had told him this attorney was the best around, and personal issues aside, he intended to hire the best. Because being forced to part with his little girl now would tear out his heart.

Even after they moved on, the encounter bugged Cody. Hallie had been quieter. Unlike the fireman, she hadn't dismissed the attorney with flippancy and teasing.

"Want to tell me why *he's* not on your list?" He wasn't sure if he wanted to hear her answer. When he looked at her, he knew he was right. "Never mind. I can see for myself."

"See what?"

"The chemistry. You're attracted to him. That's why you went all quiet on us."

Hallie was stunned by the edge in Cody's voice. And he was dead wrong. She didn't feel a sexual thing for Derek Engle. She'd gone quiet because of the look of profound love on Cody's face when he'd glanced down at his daughter. The importance of keeping that little girl with him had nearly shouted.

Looking at him now, she was surprised by the spark of anger in his steely blue eyes, uneasy with the terse set of his jaw and with the way his veins stood out on his forearms as he gripped the handle of the stroller.

If she wasn't mistaken, she'd swear Cody was jealous of Derek. That could be to her advantage, she realized. He wasn't affected by Tim, or by Brian—

even though Brian was now history. Derek, however, had caused him to react.

Maybe if she played on that a little, Cody would back off, give her space. Because space was what she needed.

It would be a big mistake to allow herself to get too comfortable in Cody's presence. He was moody. Six feet three inches of simmering passion. The promise of that passion, that danger, was thrilling. But Hallie would *not* repeat the mistakes of her mother. She *wouldn't* latch on to passion because it felt good for the moment.

She'd decided to take destiny into her hands. And when she had it firmly in her grasp, it would be a destiny guaranteed to last. A destiny that would not burn too hot, too fast, leaving behind only bitterness and ashes.

Cody's strange mood remained as they ate hamburgers and potato salad and way too much dessert. Mayor Williams gave a speech about the town and its forefathers then turned the stage and microphone over to Charlie Spangler and his country-and-western band.

Cody leaned over, his warm breath tickling her ear. "Maybe you can dance *with* me this time instead of *for* me."

"Excuse me?" Everything within her stilled at the sexual taunt in his rough tone.

"Last night, in the window."

Hallie's heart lurched and her face flamed in mortification. Oh, dear God, he'd seen her. What she'd thought had been private fantasies, harmless, had been spotlighted in all their glory by lamplight and lace curtains. She realized that now. How long had he been watching? Had she done anything weird? she wondered. Had her slip hiked up with her raised arms? How could she have lost her head that way? Danced in front of a window with the lights blazing, for goodness sake.

"You jerk!" she snapped, resorting to name calling in her total lack of composure. "I wasn't dancing for you!"

He shrugged, the dimple in his cheek creasing. "Looked that way to me."

Hallie opened her mouth, unsure of what to say, how to corral the mortification. She was saved further embarrassment as Michelle Beck came rushing over. "Come on, Hal. Let's show these folks what us nurses are made of."

Without giving her time for consent or denial, Michelle grabbed Hallie's hand and pulled her onto the civic center square.

"Well, aren't you a Little-Miss-Keep-To-Herself," the other nurse drawled. "When did Tim get replaced?"

Hallie automatically picked up the steps of the line dance. It was a minute before she could answer. Her insides were a mass of confused trembling and she felt way too hot beneath her jeans and sweater. Though she prayed fervently, no hole appeared to swallow her, to save her.

"He hasn't been replaced. Cody's my neighbor. He's been out of touch for a long time and I'm just being…neighborly." She saw him watching. Felt mortified all over again at the thought of him seeing her through the glass. His gaze tracked her as if there wasn't another woman out here. The breeze picked up, tossing her hair, sending it swirling around her head as she executed a turn in the dance.

"If he's free game, *I'd* like to be neighborly," Michelle said with a wicked grin.

Hallie narrowed her eyes. "Tony might have a thing or two to say about that."

Michelle laughed and stomped her booted heel in time with the music. "Just kidding. Besides, that man's only got eyes for you."

"Michelle, he's my *neighbor*. That's it." A spying neighbor at that.

"Whatever you say."

Charlie and the boys went into a slow rendition of "Black Velvet." The sensual strains washed over Hallie and her feet automatically picked up the steps, her eyes closing. She jolted when she felt a masculine hand at her waist.

Her eyes popped open. "Don't sneak up on me like that!"

"I'm trained to sneak." Cody moved in perfect rhythm beside her, Amy held in one strong arm. She glanced around, noticing Michelle had deserted her.

Cody's hip brushed hers. Hallie cleared her throat. "Cody, this is a line dance." *In other words, no touching. Side by side.*

"Amy wants to try it a little different." In a fluid, easy movement, he had his hand at her waist, facing her, Amy held cozily between them. Hallie's heart beat way out of proportion to any exertion she might have expended in the dance.

It was Cody's scent, the promise in his eyes, the self-confident air about him that damned convention and swept her into a dance opposite of what everyone else did on the makeshift floor.

His eyes held her, as did his hand, gently, firmly. Her feet never faltered in the rhythm, mirroring his steps as if they'd danced together for years, when in fact this was the first time.

She gave a thought to the picture they made, a man and a woman with a baby between them, gliding easily to the sensual beat, neither speaking. At least not with their mouths. Their eyes spoke volumes…asking, answering, wanting yet denying.

"Say yes, Slick."

She knew what he was asking. To take their relationship into intimacy. She shook her head.

"I could change your mind."

"You probably could. But I'd be sorry."

She saw his sensual mouth tighten, felt his fingers bite into her waist. Amy laid her head on Cody's shoulder, her solemn unblinking eyes fixed steadily on Hallie, a mirror of her father's. Then she stuck her thumb in her mouth and reached for Hallie. Hallie couldn't deny the little girl. She stepped into the hug, placing a soft kiss on Amy's sweet-smelling cheek.

Her thighs brushed Cody's. He took advantage of the moment and drew her closer. Their bodies pressed and moved as one. Hallie ached to give in, to take that walk on the wild side that his steady gaze promised. It would be good. There was no doubt about that. But she couldn't. And because she couldn't let herself, the feelings were all the more bittersweet, the wanting all the more fierce.

For some unaccountable reason, she wanted to cry. With Amy's head occupying one of Cody's strong shoulders, Hallie rested her forehead on the other. He smelled of baby powder and mustard and forbidden desire. A strange combination, a combination that made her insides tremble.

When the music wound down, Hallie was barely aware. She realized that Cody's feet had stopped—and she heard applause.

Startled, she jerked back and looked around. They were the only two people on the makeshift dance floor.

Charlie's voice boomed over the microphone. "Let's hear it for slow dancin'! Best darn rendition of 'Black Velvet' I've ever seen! Maybe those two will agree to give lessons."

Embarrassed, terribly afraid the desire trembling inside of her was radiating like a beacon, Hallie drew in a deep breath, plastered a smile on her face, and executed a gracious bow. "Take a bow, Cody. You're a hit."

He flashed his sexy, bad-boy grin and every woman in the crowd nearly swooned. Who in their right mind could resist a dark-haired rebel tenderly cradling a baby in his arms?

"Folks," Charlie added over the speaker system, "for those of you that don't know him, that's Cody Brock and his little daughter. He's settling back here in Parkdale. Be sure and make him welcome."

"Hallie seems to be doing a fairly good job of that," came a female voice out of the crowd.

Hallie searched for the woman behind the voice and found her. Jeanie Atkins. Cody's high school bleacher girl. Hallie raised a brow and stared right back at Jeanie.

Raising her voice, she said, "Yeah, but you can't expect me to do it all. I'm sure Cody would appreciate a few invitations for some home-cooked meals."

"I'm offering," shouted Trina Lorry. She was widowed and twice Cody's age. The crowd laughed.

Cody grinned and hollered right back. "I accept, ma'am." From the side of his mouth, he whispered, "Thanks a lot, Slick."

"You're welcome," she said sweetly. "I'd hate to see your appetite suffer." The minute the words were out, she regretted them.

"My appetite's not for food right now and you damned well know it."

Realizing she'd backed herself into a corner, she reached for Amy, using the little girl as a shield, and danced off into the crowd, joining Michelle and Terri, the nurses from Parkdale General. The three women cooed over the baby.

Unable to help herself, her gaze sought out Cody's. Even from a distance, she could read his expression clearly. The slightest smirk tilted his sculpted lips.

You can run, baby, his eyes seemed to say. *But not forever.*

Trembling, heart pounding, she dragged her gaze away.

Chapter Ten

Amy didn't even stir when Hallie took her out of the
car seat.

"You've got a great touch, Slick."

She followed him to the house, waiting while he
unlocked the door. The breeze had turned chill.
Clouds clustered together like angry guardians and
thunder rumbled off in the distance. They were in for
a storm. Perfect weather for the way Hallie was feeling. Stormy. Edgy.

And Cody wasn't helping that uneasiness. He
watched her with a probing intensity that made her
tremble. She didn't want to go in with him. Because
if she took that step over the threshold with the way
she was feeling, she feared she'd never want to leave.

"Do you want me to take her?" she asked. Aware-
ness shivered between them, over the top of the sleeping baby's head.

She shook her head. "No sense disturbing her."

He nodded. "You're right. I don't want to wake
her. Not tonight."

He stepped into the house. Hallie had little choice

but to follow. There'd been a dangerous promise underlying his words, a warning. Her heart pounded and her conscience waged a battle. A battle she desperately wanted to lose.

Once she had Amy in the crib, Hallie slipped off the baby's pink-and-white tennis shoes and covered her with a blanket.

"She should be okay sleeping in her sweats." Hallie whispered, glad she'd insisted Cody dress his daughter for comfort rather than fashion.

Finished with her task, she turned. Cody still watched her. Silently. Solemnly.

Nerves threatened her composure. "Well...I guess I'll get going."

For a minute she thought he wasn't going to move aside so she could pass. Then he stepped back and shut off the light, leaving Amy's room in the soft glow of a night-light shaped like a duck.

"What's your hurry, Slick?"

"I should get home before the rain starts."

"It'll hold off for a while." He touched her shoulder, making her jolt. "I want to show you something. Will you come with me?" he asked softly.

Hallie hesitated then nodded, drawn despite herself by the fleeting glimpse of uncertainty she'd seen in his blue eyes.

He led the way to his drafting table. "Harlan and Darby have taken on some new friends. My editor likes them. I'd like your opinion."

She didn't have an opinion in her head right now. Looking at Cody, all she could think about was how the lamplight turned his hair blue-black and darkened his eyes to indigo, eyes that studied her with a power that jarred. Her hands shook and her insides quaked. Pulling her gaze away, she focused on his story-boards.

Her eyes widened. "I have *never* worn a mini-skirted nurse's uniform!"

Cody's lips tilted, slowly, sensually. "Try it some-time. It'll make your male patients happy and the fe-male ones envious."

"That's a terribly sexist thing to say. Besides, my patients are little kids. I doubt they'd notice." She studied the drawing. The character had more curves than she did, but otherwise was kind of cute. She wore roller skates and balanced a cake with a single hand.

"Am I being presumptuous, or is this really me?"

"It's based on you...and Amy." The baby was pic-tured on all fours, crawling after the nurse, diapers drooping.

Hallie flipped through the drawings. There was a strip depicting their meals-on-wheels outing. And one of Harlan juggling apples in the grocery store as the nurse and baby looked on in admiration and Darby rolled his eyes, proclaiming Harlan a show-off.

Hallie wondered if the Founders Day trip would show up tomorrow. Like he'd done with his buddy in the service, Cody seemed to be drawing *their* daily experiences.

Cody felt vulnerable as Hallie examined his sketches. Funny how he never thought about the fact that millions saw these cartoons, yet when Hallie touched them, studied them, he held his breath, worried that she'd judge him and find him lacking.

He knew she'd been about to bolt and had grabbed at any excuse to keep her with him. Being so close to her all evening, touching her, breathing in her scent, had driven him wild. Now, it wasn't Amy's erratic sleeping habits that kept him up at nights. It was thoughts of Hallie.

She turned, caught him staring and went very still. She wanted him. He could see it in the pulse at her throat, in her brown eyes that had suddenly dilated to near black, saw the desire in the shimmering, moist part of her lips.

Her hands were unsteady, clenched at her sides as if held there to keep from reaching out.

"I won't make it easy for you to walk away from me tonight." He stepped closer, crowding her, tempting her.

The past few days had taken their toll on him. Watching that erotic, solo dance...dancing with her tonight. Touching her. If she didn't stay with him he thought he'd die. He couldn't lose her before he'd even had a chance to hold her, to show her how it could be between them.

I'd be sorry. Her words echoed back at him. He'd make damned sure she wasn't.

"You won't regret it, Hallie. Say yes."

Hallie looked up at him, surrounded by his size, his power, wanting to accept what she knew he offered, yet knowing it was wrong, knowing that with change disaster often followed. "Cody, I don't want to lose your friendship."

He didn't say a word. He simply kissed her, slow and soft and deep so that the protest slid back down her throat. Her world narrowed, centering solely on Cody, on his touch, his lips, the flavor that was so uniquely his. She couldn't move, couldn't think, but knew she must. For if she allowed this to continue, it would only take one breath, one word, to start the hope in her heart.

A love that wasn't meant to be.

His fingers tunneled through her hair, easing her head back, gently forcing her gaze to his.

"You'll never lose my friendship, sweetheart. Please say yes."

And in that instant, Hallie knew it was too late. She'd already taken that breath, heard that word, felt the hope soar in her heart.

Just this once, she bargained with herself. A conscious choice to feel, to taste the forbidden. A memory to hold in her heart. She'd never wanted a man more than she wanted Cody, and the thought of facing the rest of her life knowing she hadn't had the courage to reach out and seize what she wanted was unthinkable.

"I'm not making any promises, Cody."

"I'm not asking for promises. Just permission."

It would have been easier if he'd just taken the choice from her, swept her into desire, to a place where there were no thoughts. Just feelings, sensations.

But he wasn't going to make it easy for her. Whatever happened between them this night she'd have to take full responsibility for.

She heard him groan, low and deep in his throat when her arms lifted to his shoulders, her fingers twining in his hair. She no longer cared if making love with Cody wasn't right. She had to have his arms around her, ached to feel what it would be like to have all of him inside her, to culminate the powerful rush that had begun fifteen years ago.

Forbidden love.

A tantalizing, erotic walk on the wild side.

Maybe it was wrong, but right now, at this moment, it felt so right. She wanted to feel his caress. Needed it with an urgency that burned in her soul.

His palms framed her face, his fingertips tracing, mapping, worshiping, as if he were learning every last detail of her being, as if her secrets told their story in braille. So gentle. So erotic. She felt as if a hot cord ran through her body, pumping electricity from her heart to her femininity. And all the while, as he touched, as he seduced, his intense eyes never left her face.

The moment spun out endlessly. She heard music, a tinkling sound. Not coins. More like the clink of bangle bracelets chiming together. Or the jingle of a tiny bell around a monkey's neck. Mystical. Magical.

Sabrina's image flashed before her mind. A warning? A gentle nudge to keep her on track? To keep her from teetering over the edge of the forbidden, the edge of madness?

The shadowy, whisper of sound tinkled again, farther away this time. Her heart thudded. Both from uncertainty and from the erotic path of Cody's lips.

"Did you hear that?"

"Bells?" he murmured against her neck. "I told you we'd be good together."

"No," she breathed, having trouble with her concentration. "Did you *hear* it."

"I always hear bells when I look at you. When I touch you."

He was speaking figuratively. Humoring her. Two weeks ago she'd seen visions that weren't there. Now she was hearing sounds.

"It's probably just Amy's jingle bear," she mused. "Maybe it fell out of the crib."

"Slick?"

"Hmm?" His clever tongue did amazing things to her ear, making her shiver.

"I'm trying to make love to you here. Suppose we could have a little concentration?"

"I'm..." She sucked in a breath as his thumb brushed the underside of her breast. "Definitely concentrating," she said on a shaky exhale.

He eased back, studying her. A charged connection held their eyes. Emotions barely checked poured out of him, straight into her, silently speaking to every forbidden impulse she'd ever had. Impulses she'd never even known existed before Cody.

His hand eased up her throat, the leashed power frightening her, thrilling her.

"Poor planning." His voice rasped, low and deep.

"What?"

"We should be doing this with your music playing. 'The Principles of Lust' was it called? Damn, Slick. I nearly died watching you."

And she nearly died each time he reminded her. The zing of embarrassment vied with the words he'd just spoken.

Lust, he'd said. Not love.

She almost came to her senses but Cody's hand moved, slowly, erotically, from her throat to the buttons of her blouse, releasing them, laying the material open. Her nipples pebbled in anticipation. Strong, blunt fingers dispatched the front snap of her bra with an expertise that made her tremble.

"You're beautiful." He traced the outline of her breasts, coming so close, yet never touching the aching center. "So soft. So warm."

She wanted him to hurry, thought to tell him as much, but his mouth swept all rational thought from her head, shooting her into a maelstrom of desire so fierce she could hardly remember her name.

Instead of pulling away as she should have, Hallie arched closer, seeking his lips, his tongue, trembling in anticipation, welcoming him with actions older than time.

She pressed her hips against him, needing the pressure, needing…something, anything to put out the fire running rampant through her body.

He lifted her in his arms, his lips never breaking contact, cementing her fantasies. No man had ever carried her, holding her as if she were more precious than gold.

She had little time to notice anything about his bedroom other than the king-size bed that dominated. He laid her on the rumpled sheets and followed, his weight pressing her down, making her burn hotter than the fires of hell.

Thunder burst from the heavens and lightning streaked the sky. The first drops of rain began to fall, pelting the windowpanes. The sounds of the storm outside released a wildness in Hallie.

She didn't even begin to know the woman she'd become, had no idea the madness existed. Teetering on the brink of something wonderful, something forbidden, something so elemental it hurt, she tugged at his shirt with one hand and reached for his belt with the other. He obliged her with the shirt, but drew back when her hands touched the front of his jeans.

"I've waited a long time for you, Slick. All my life, it seems. I won't hurry."

"But...I want you to hurry. I need..." Her stomach dipped as his finger traced a path low on her abdomen, parting her zipper, easing her jeans down her legs.

"What do you want?" His hand cupped her through the silk of her panties, just for an instant, then smoothed over her hip, teasing, torturing. "How do you want it?"

Hot and wild. Her face flamed even though she hadn't uttered the words. "Cody, just do it."

His eyes narrowed. "You want to feel the touch of a bad boy, is that it?"

Yes! She nearly screamed the word, but it remained locked in her throat. His finger traced her femininity now, a featherlight touch that nearly sent her over the edge.

"Is that what you want?" he asked again.

She nodded but his hand stilled, confusing her, drawing forth a groan of protest.

"Is that what this is about, Slick? Are you satisfying your curiosity?"

She shook her head. "No. Cody, I want you. Just you." Now. Oh, God, she couldn't stand the sweet torture a second longer.

"Which me?" he persisted.

"I don't know what you mean."

"I think you do. But I don't think I'll give you what you're asking for. You wouldn't like it."

"Yes I would."

"You want to be *taken*? Not this time. This time is for you. All for you. Everything I have to *give*."

Something in his tone penetrated her hazy mind. She'd touched a sensitive cord in him. She should have realized. Just as she'd fantasized about him, about the magnetism of a brooding rebel, so had plenty of other women. Cody was the type of man women would throw themselves at, hoping to be the one to tame him. He'd been treated like a trophy. A prize. A challenge.

And she was asking for a taste of the same.

Cody stood and unbuckled his belt, kicking off his

shoes and his jeans. He'd always been comfortable with his nudity, never really given much thought to what women saw in his body.

He thought about it now. Hallie's gaze was both curious and blatant, making him glad he kept up a regular exercise regimen.

When her gaze finally lifted back to his eyes, he was achingly hard. He needed control, reached deep for it. Otherwise this would all be over with in a matter of three minutes and blow his image all to hell.

He eased back down on the bed, kissing her eyelids, her temple, wanting to rush, *needing* to rush, yet taking his time. Plenty of time.

With hands and lips he mapped her body, gauging her level of desire, watching, taking her up to a feverish pitch then gently easing her down.

She groaned, reached for him, but he evaded her hands.

"All night," he whispered, praying to God he could last. He wanted to call the shots, wanted to make sure that any thoughts or experiences she'd had with other men were wiped from her mind. Replaced only by him.

This was virgin territory for him. In the past when he'd taken a woman to bed, he'd only looked for instant gratification. Women had courted him, intrigued by his silence, his image. That had been fine with him. He'd never wanted any strings to bind him.

But Hallie was different. With her, he *wanted* strings. Wanted them wound so tight she'd never escape.

"Cody, please," she begged, gripping the back of his head as his tongue circled the incredibly smooth skin of her breast. There wasn't an inch of her body he hadn't worshiped, with both fingers and tongue. Yet just when she teetered on the edge of madness, he drew back, soothing, then inflaming again, giving every detailed section of her body his rapt attention.

Watching her spiraling desire fed his own. He'd never known such intensity existed. Never.

Hallie couldn't take it anymore. She shifted, trying to urge him on top of her, trying to reach him, to touch him, to return the erotic ministrations that were driving her insane.

Her body was on fire, throbbing, aching, pulsing with a beat that left her dizzy.

"Say my name again," he demanded.

"Cody," she panted.

"Good."

He slid down her body. She thought to stop him, to plead with him, yet within seconds he brought her to a climax with his mouth that was so explosively exquisite she nearly fainted. Then his fingers replaced his lips, prolonging the tremors, threatening her sanity.

"Now! Cody, now."

"Yes." He ripped the foil of a prophylactic with his teeth. Their hands tangled together as she tried to help, urging him to hurry, shifting to make room for him between her legs. At last she felt him pressed against her, teasing, torturing.

"I don't share, Hallie."

"No," she cried, not understanding his possessive words, beyond even caring. The world could come to an end right now and she wouldn't care. She had to have him now. All of him. Inside her. She arched up at the same moment he thrust forward.

"Oh," she cried. "It's been so long. So good."

He went very still, letting her adjust to his fullness. She gripped him with her legs, urging him to move. The sensations were too much. And not nearly enough.

"How long, Slick?"

"Ages. Now, Cody. Now."

Whatever control Cody had prided himself on fled with her impassioned plea. She was every fantasy he'd ever dreamed of. Responsive. Avid in her participation. She met his thrusts, breath heaving, her nails biting into his shoulders, her hips rotating in a way that drove him wild, pressed him clear to the back of her womb.

He didn't know how much longer he could last. Sweat beaded at his temples, prickled all along his skin. His teeth ground together. She was tight and slick and hot. He felt his release building, prayed for control, prayed like he'd never prayed before.

"Let...go, baby."

She cried out. He felt her muscles clench around him, saw the flush stain her chest and neck, marveled at the look of utter ecstasy on her beautiful features. His own release slammed into him with the force of a charging bull, uncivilized, powerful, hurtling him over the edge of a peak so high he thought he'd shatter.

As HER SENSES slowly returned to reality, Hallie shut her eyes. What had she done? A rush of embarrassment flooded her because of her complete loss of control, her utter wanton behavior.

She finally understood the irresistible pull of passion, the wild emotions that tied a woman in knots, tempted her to make impulsive choices.

This had definitely been an impulsive choice. Explosively impulsive.

She eased out of his hold and sat up.

"Where are you going?"

"Home."

"Slick?"

She glanced at him feeling naked. Not just unclothed naked, but vulnerable. The bedside clock read 12:30 a.m.

"It's my birthday," she whispered.

"Today was?"

"No. Today as in Sunday. Yesterday's already gone." And she couldn't turn back the clock. Couldn't undo what had been done in this bed. She needed to get out of here. Get her head on straight.

She couldn't repeat the mistakes of her mother.

"We should go out, or something," Cody said. "Celebrate."

Swinging her legs over the side of the bed, she stepped into her jeans and snatched up her blouse, not bothering with her bra. "I've got plans."

He went very still behind her.

"Change them."

"I can't. Tim's already arranged a party at the steak house."

"The suit," he sneered. "What the hell is the matter with you?"

She glanced uneasily at him as he swore and got out of the bed, jerking his jeans on. His belt hung open, as did the snap at his waist. Shirtless, he looked like a dark, avenging warrior.

Hallie didn't trust this mood. She saw his nostrils flair, heard his breathing. Lightning streaked past the window and thunder boomed, making her jump like a startled rabbit. She'd seen that same look on her father's face countless times, seen both her parents squared off in anger. Passionate anger.

Then the yelling would begin, faults dredged up and old history rehashed. After several rounds, her father would invariably storm out of the house, abandoning Hallie's mother. Abandoning her.

Abandonment brought on by passion.

This time, Hallie wasn't going to wait around for heartbreak and tears. This time, *she* was going to be the one to walk. It was her only means of control.

"I've got to go, Cody."

"You're joking, right?"

She shook her head and picked up her shoes without putting them on.

"Didn't what we just did in that bed mean anything to you? Or was I right? Did you just want to check out a rebel's technique between the sheets?"

"Don't be ugly, Cody. I didn't plan this."

"Oh, that's right. I forgot about your plans. Your chart."

Guilt swamped her, tightening her throat. Probably because most of what Cody said was right. She just didn't like admitting it. She *had* wanted to take a walk on the wild side, just this once, when all the while her plans were for something completely different.

With a different man.

Not Cody. Tim.

She had to get out of here before she did something even more stupid and cried. Her stomach was twisted in knots. Tim had gone out of town and she'd betrayed him.

For passion.

Which just proved that passion caused nothing but trouble.

She felt the tears sting and blinked furiously.

"Slick?" His voice had softened in concern. An angry Cody, she could deal with. The man who read children's books to his baby daughter and drew cartoons of best friends, and took time to soothe the aches of a teenage girl in emotional pain was an entirely different matter.

"I'm sorry, Cody. I'm so sorry."

She whirled and fled the room, out of the house and into the storm. The storm that drenched her with chill rain, blending with her tears.

Tears for a love that wasn't meant to be. A love that she couldn't *allow* to be.

Chapter Eleven

Tim picked her up promptly at seven. Hallie halfway expected Cody to show up at the door with some lame excuse to delay her.

She hadn't seen him all day, except from a distance. Twice. Once when he'd left with Amy in the Blazer. Again when he'd returned. He hadn't even looked in the direction of her house—she'd been watching. He hadn't called to wish her a happy birthday. Then again, why would he after the way they'd parted?

Tim leaned down and placed a sweet kiss on her lips. It moved her about as much as kissing her brother—assuming she had a brother. She felt guilty and leaned into him, determined to feel…something.

Her chest came up against a package he held in his hand.

"Happy birthday," Tim said.

"Oh." She straightened and accepted the gift he held out. "Thank you. Should I open it now?"

"Of course. It is the day, isn't it? The big three-oh?"

Hallie smiled and punched him lightly on the shoulder. "I wish you wouldn't remind me."

She sat on the couch and tore into the paper. *Jingle, clink. Jingle, clink.* The coins in his pocket sifted together annoyingly as he stood there watching her.

Her stomach muscles clenched at the aggravating habit.

With the wrapping paper half torn off, she jumped to her feet and retrieved the coffee can she'd decorated with sunflowers.

"Sounds like you have a pocket full of change," she said brightly. "Care to contribute to my cause?" She held out the can.

"Sure. What's the cause."

"It's a donation jar I've started for the ladies' auxiliary. I've got a few ideas for fund-raisers." Like emptying Tim's pockets every other day.

"Great idea." He pulled out his wallet. Hallie's spirits sank.

"Save your bills, Tim. This jar's only for change."

He frowned. "Seems unbalanced to me. I was going to drop in a twenty. In change, I've only got a dollar or so."

"That's fine," she assured with what she hoped was an innocent smile. "Besides, you might need your dollars to tip the cocktail waitress."

"Oh. sure." He dropped his coins into the open can she held out. Reluctantly, it seemed.

He really was a good man, Hallie thought, handsome, tall and rangy, sandy hair styled fashionably short. He wore dress pants, a long-sleeve shirt and a subtly striped tie. Hallie felt underdressed in her jeans, cotton blouse and cowboy boots. But the get-together was for country-and-western dancing.

"Thanks, Tim."

"Okay. Finish opening your present. I've got a responsibility to get the birthday girl to the party on time."

The box was flat and square. She pried it open at the corners.

And stared.

A piece of folding cardboard with slots for coins. And a book on coin collections and their value.

"Oh. How…wonderful." Her lips stretched into a smile. She knew absolutely nothing about coins—except for how they grated on her nerves when jangled together in a man's pocket. "Thank you, Tim."

"I'll give you a couple of coins from my collection to get you started. Then you're on your own."

It's the thought behind the gift, she told herself. Not the gift itself. She put a little more effort behind her smile this time.

"A start for the future. This really is great, Tim. Like saving for a rainy day…or a child's college education."

He grinned and held out his hand, helping her to her feet. "Perfect."

THE NOISE LEVEL in the steak house was deafening. The nurses from Parkdale General had pooled their money and rented a jukebox filled with country-and-western compact discs. As the liquor flowed, the volume increased.

"Looks like your date's arguing with the waitress," Michelle said, clapping and stomping to the boot-scootin' boogie.

From her position on the dance floor, Hallie glanced at their table, frowning. Tim never lost his cool. Why would he be arguing with Crissy Metz?

The song ended and Hallie said, "I've got to sit down. I'm bushed."

"Yeah. That happens when you get to be an old lady of thirty."

"Every dog has her day, Michelle. If I'm not mistaken, yours will be next spring. And your respirations are a little shallow, so I wouldn't talk."

"My respirations may be shallow but my ticker's aerobically sound."

"Then by all means, stay and dance."

"Oh, no," Michelle teased. "What kind of a friend would I be if I didn't help an old lady back to her table?" She gripped Hallie's elbow and Hallie burst out laughing.

They were still cracking up and clowning around when they got back to the table. Hallie scooted her chair closer to Tim. The waitress was nowhere in sight.

"Weren't you just talking to Crissy?" Hallie asked.

Tim jerked and knocked over his glass of champagne. The liquid ran off the table and into his lap before he could leap out of the way. Hallie snatched up napkins, mopping up the mess. Before she even thought about her actions, she swiped at the front of Tim's pants, trying to soak up the bulk of the liquid.

It was at that instant that she looked up and saw Cody.

Eye level with Tim's belt buckle and sopping pants, she felt her face flame. She closed her eyes and handed Tim the napkin.

"Here. You'd better do that."

He appeared about as embarrassed as she was. The waitress, Crissy, showed up with a fluffy white towel and another tray of drinks. "Uh, I'll just go to the men's room," Tim said, excusing himself.

Her heart pounding like a drum, she raised her gaze, watching as Cody wove his way between the tables of the bar. His stride as well as his stature commanded the attention of every female in the room— and quite a few of the males.

He wore jeans and boots and a tight black T-shirt. Not exactly country-and-western attire, but more appropriate than Tim's preppy business look.

A lock of hair fell over his forehead as he stopped at a table a few feet away and bent over to talk to Charlie Spangler. His sculpted lips flashed a sexy smile at the young brunette sitting with Charlie.

Jealousy grabbed Hallie right in the heart. Which was perfectly ridiculous. She didn't have a claim on the man.

Dragging her gaze away, she stared at the diet soda on the table in front of her as if it were the most fascinating object.

She felt his body heat before he even spoke. Smelled his masculine scent.

His fingers wrapped around the back of her chair, brushing her back, sending shivers up her spine. He leaned down, his lips a heartbeat away from her ear.

"Happy birthday, Slick." The music playing drowned out his words to all but her. She barely suppressed the shiver that his warm breath created.

Hallie cleared her throat. "Cody. I didn't know you'd be here."

"Wouldn't be very *friendly* of me to miss your birthday celebration."

She glanced at him sharply when he stressed the word *friendly*. His masculine face was a study of innocence. As if one could ever call Cody Brock innocent. Heartthrob, yes. Dangerous, yes. But innocent? His blue eyes could melt a woman on the spot. They'd certainly melted her.

"Where's Amy?"

"Hazel and George are watching her."

"Yikes."

He grinned, sending her pulse rate skittering. "If I didn't trust them completely, I wouldn't be here. Is this seat taken?" He pulled out the chair Tim had vacated.

"Uh, Tim is…he'll be back from the men's room in a minute."

"This seat's not occupied," Michelle volunteered, pointing to the vacant one between her and Lisa Garmetti.

"Thanks. Michelle, wasn't it?"

Hallie could see Michelle's pleasure that Cody remembered her name. She felt duty bound to mention her friend's fiancé again but held her tongue. Michelle flirted with everybody but was true-blue to her beau.

Lisa, on the other hand, was unattached and clearly setting her sights on Cody.

Hallie shot Cody a you-can-leave-anytime-now look. The damned man merely winked at her.

Tim returned to the table, the front of his pants still damp. Hallie slipped her arm through his and leaned close. "Would you like to dance?"

"No, I'm fine. You go ahead, though. It's your birthday. Have a good time."

She could have socked him. Where was his gallantry? Didn't he realize another man was sitting at their table? A man who was alternately staring at her and at the furniture between them as if he were testing its suitability for sexual purposes? Didn't he realize the other man sitting there doing a credible James Dean imitation was someone she'd gone to bed with?

No. Obviously he didn't. He appeared oblivious to Cody's presence. And Cody, in turn, dismissed Tim as if he weren't even there. This was awkward.

Hallie couldn't stop the groan that escaped. Tim leaned closer, inquiring after her health. Cody leaned farther back in his chair, tipping it on two legs, and smirked.

"I'm perfectly fine," she said to the table at large. "Michelle, my love, would you care to dance?"

"Does a pig have a snout? Let's go, girl."

The lively number was just what Hallie needed to expend her energy, to take her mind off Cody Brock.

Until she saw him being led onto the dance floor by Lisa.

Cuddly, curvy, *available* Lisa.

She whirled toward Michelle, turning her back on the sight, hiding her misery behind a bright smile.

"I wouldn't worry," Michelle said.

"Who say's I'm worried? I told you, he's just my neighbor."

"I was talking about Tim not wanting to dance. Guess we know where your mind is."

Hallie rolled her eyes. "You know Tim's not a dancer."

Michelle seemed about to say something, then changed her mind. "Lucky for you I love it. And lucky for you I know when to dance across the room."

"What?" She felt a masculine shoulder brush hers and knew without looking that it was Cody. He didn't say a word, just fell in with the steps of the line dance, his body brushing her side with each shuffle step.

Hallie stared straight ahead, focusing her gaze on Tim. Safe Tim. The perfect boy-next-door-*type,* Tim. She saw him smile at her and lift his glass in salute.

The guilt nearly undid her. She missed a step, zigged when she should have zagged and ran smack into Cody, nearly causing a pileup on the dance floor.

Lisa, who danced on Cody's other side, shot Hallie an annoyed look.

Cody chuckled, his hand shooting out to steady

Hallie, to guide her back into step with the rest of the dancers. Hallie felt tears burn the back of her eyes— her nerves were shot to hell.

He must have felt her distress. His hand eased down her arm. For a split instant, his fingers twined with hers, squeezing softly. "Want to sit this one out?"

She nodded and moved off the dance floor. Cody didn't follow right away. The fact that he didn't increased her guilt. She felt sneaky, as if they'd engaged in a tryst and were trying to make it look innocent.

Which pretty much summed things up in a nutshell.

"Having a good time?" Tim asked as she slid into the chair next to him.

"Yes." *No. I'm miserable.* "Thank you for arranging this."

When the song ended, Cody came back to their table, but didn't sit down. He held out his hand to Tim. "Cody Brock." His gaze shifted to Hallie. She knew he was just itching to tack on "cartoonist." Thankfully he refrained.

"We met at Hallie's," he reminded.

"Yes, of course," Tim said, turning up the wattage of his banker smile. "Are you settled in now?"

"Getting there."

"Well, I'm sure if you need anything you can call on Hallie. She's a great one to have for a neighbor. Very giving."

"Very," Cody murmured.

Hallie jolted, mortified, and nearly slid under the

table. She was almost sure that *Two-timer* was flashing across her forehead.

Of course it wasn't. And of course no one else at the table realized that Tim's interpretation of *giving* and Cody's were light-years apart.

Cody turned and held out his hand to Hallie. She had little choice but to take it, allowing him to enfold hers between both his palms. He tugged slightly, pulling her forward as he bent.

"Happy birthday," he said loud enough for everyone at the table to hear. Instead of straightening like she thought he would, he just kept coming, until his lips were a breath away from her ear. "The *suit* gets a minus ten for attentiveness."

She sucked in a breath.

"I'm keeping score," he whispered, his lips brushing her cheek in a soft kiss. To an onlooker it was merely the kiss of an acquaintance. Friendly. No big deal. Half the men in this room had given her such a kiss.

But to Hallie it was more. Much, much more.

He walked out alone. Just like he'd been most of his life. For an insane moment, she wanted to run after him, to make sure he wasn't ever alone again.

She couldn't. He wasn't her destiny. She wouldn't let him be. He was a man who had the power to break her heart. A man who exuded a passion so enticing, she'd compromise anything to share in just one small part of it.

And that was simply too dangerous a prospect to even consider.

WHEN TIM WALKED HER to the door, it was after midnight. The porch light shone in welcome. It was a house that had seen sad times and a lot of fighting. She had the power to change all that. She could fill this house with gentle love and happy children. A husband who went to work at eight and came home at five. A safe, easy life.

On the other hand, maybe she'd just sell the place and move into Tim's condominium. It would certainly solve her problem of having to see Cody day in and day out. To eliminate the temptation.

"Did you enjoy your evening?" Tim asked.

Hallie smiled and placed her palm on his shirtfront. As milestone birthdays went, this one had been fairly anticlimactic, but it had been nice.

"Yes, I did." Her palm smoothed higher on his chest, slipping under his tie.

"Hey, more gifts," Tim commented, leaning down to lift a package that was sitting by the door.

Hallie's hand dropped like a rock. Well, so what if the guy didn't recognize a subtle come-on when he saw one. Not everybody was as oversexed as her neighbor!

Tim handed her the brightly wrapped gift, apparently not the least bit curious about who'd left it on the porch.

She couldn't help thinking that if this had been Cody, he'd have wanted to know the gift giver's name, the contents and why the person didn't have the nerve to deliver it in person.

She turned the package over looking for a card. There wasn't one. "I wonder who it's from."

"Probably a secret admirer," Tim said hooking his arm lightly over her shoulder. "You do so much for the people in this community. I bet half the town's in love with you."

She waited with both dread and anticipation, wondering if he'd include himself among the people who cared so much about her. A part of her wanted him to. He was the right choice. Her scorecard even proved it.

He brushed his lips against hers. It was a nice kiss, a neat kiss, gentle and soft, yet firm.

Not a single spark of fire ignited in her belly.

Guilt slammed into her when she realized she'd automatically compared Tim's polite technique to Cody's erotic style.

For crying out loud, now she was reduced to rating kisses. Where was the spontaneity of attraction?

Tied up with Cody Brock, she realized.

The wrong guy.

She was more mixed up than a woman should be on her thirtieth birthday. She felt like a two-timer.

But who was she two-timing? Tim? Or Cody?

"'Night, pretty lady," Tim said.

"Good night, Tim."

Letting herself into the quiet house, she sank down onto the sofa and fingered the yellow ribbon taped to the sunflower wrapping paper. Was it from Cody?

She traced the petals of the happy flowers and nearly shrieked when the phone rang.

Heart pounding, she hesitated, then took a deep breath and picked up the receiver.

"Hello?"

"Hey, cuz'. How's it feel to be an old hag?"

"Maggie!" She'd have known that deep-throated Texas drawl anywhere.

"Yeah. Happy Birthday."

"Oh, Mag, I'm glad you remembered."

"Of course I remembered. What's up with you? You don't sound very chipper for a birthday girl."

"It's after midnight, Maggie. And my ears are still ringing from the loud music."

"Been honky-tonking?"

"Absolutely.

"Good for you. By the way, I heard from Clarissa. She's back in Bridgeport."

"I know," Hallie said. "Seems I've been playing phone tag with both of you. Every time I call, you're not there and vice versa."

"I'm glad I got you tonight," Maggie said, then hesitated. "Funny thing, happened. Clarissa and I got to talking and realized both of us had seen Sabrina. On Labor Day."

Hallie felt that eerie sense of expectancy again. Magical. Scary. "Maggie," she whispered into the receiver. "I saw her, too. On Labor Day." She paused. "It's weird, though. I thought I'd hallucinated or something. She was in an old-fashioned gypsy wagon. At my front curb."

She waited for a peal of laughter, for an admonishment that she'd lost her mind. But Maggie, ever unflappable, simply said, "I saw her in Manhattan."

Hallie's grip tightened on the receiver. "I suppose it's not impossible, but it sure is strange."

"Clarissa saw her in Chicago. At the Bridgeport festival."

Chills went straight up Hallie's spine. She heard the faint tinkling of bells and whipped around, her heart hammering. The house was quiet. She was alone.

Except for her cousin on the other end of the phone line. "What, Maggie? I missed what you said."

"I said, there's magic in the air. Destiny."

Something was going on here. She could hear it in her cousin's tone. Hallie's voice softened, inviting confidence. "Have you found your destiny in Texas, Mag?"

Maggie laughed. "I'm working on it."

"Does *it* have a name?"

"Maybe."

"And?" Hallie prompted. She'd never known her cousin to be so secretive. She could usually count on Maggie to spill her guts with little or no prompting. "Don't leave me hanging like this."

"I think I will. If this is magic, I don't want to jinx it. How about you. Anything or *anyone* new on the horizon?"

Cody's image flashed before her mind, tall and tough, with a bad-boy smile that could coax a nun right out of her sensible robes. She didn't dare mention his name, though, because Maggie would want to know the details. And her cousin was awfully good at getting Hallie to tell all.

Right now, her feelings for Cody were too raw, too forbidden to take out and examine.

So Hallie took the true coward's route and said, "Nothing magical on my horizon. At least not yet. My scorecard's leaning toward the bank manager here in town. I'll keep you posted on the progress."

"Hal?"

"Yes?"

"You're lying like a dog."

Hallie couldn't prevent the bubble of laughter that spilled out. "Oh, I'm crazy about you, Mag. 'Night. Thanks for calling."

She hung up the phone and curled her legs beneath her on the couch, wishing Maggie was here instead of in Texas, wishing they could spend the whole night talking. Just like they used to when they were girls. Clarissa, Maggie and Hallie. There hadn't been a problem in the world the three of them couldn't solve together.

Her knee brushed against the package and she lifted it, running her fingertips over the paper, prolonging the suspense. Finally, she slipped the yellow ribbon off and ran her nail along the seam of the tape, carefully preserving the paper.

Lifting the lid, she pushed aside the tissue paper and felt tears spill over her eyelashes.

Sunflower babies. Little wooden dolls with straw hair and ribbons and aprons.

He'd sketched a miniature version of his cartoon

strip on the card. Harlan, wearing Marine fatigues and his signature leather jacket, looking uncomfortable as he handed a package to the nurse wearing a miniskirt and roller skates. The nerd hid behind a building, peeking around the corner, an open book in his hands proclaiming Proper Steps to Courting Etiquette with a subtitle of Birthdays. The baby, graduated now from crawling to unsteady first steps, peeked between Harlan's legs, her little hands fisted on his pant leg.

The dialogue bubble above the hoodlum said, "The kid saw this and thought you'd like it."

In the next frame, the nurse's eyes widened, clearly pleased, Harlan looked relieved and Darby leapt into the air, fist raised, book flying, shouting, "Ooo-rah, pal! That's a Pro ten points on the chart!"

Hallie smiled through her tears. Ooo-rah in Marine jargon meant "way to go."

Below the cartoon strip, Cody had simply written, "Happy Birthday, Slick."

She traced the last line of the card with her fingertip. Yes, a gift thoughtfully chosen would constitute a Pro.

But Cody wasn't on her list. Well, technically his name was still in her spiral notebook. She hadn't been able to bring herself to rip out the page. Somehow, the mere thought of the action felt like a rend to her heart.

Her head was what she should be listening to though, because in her head, she knew what was right. She wanted a guy who'd guarantee her smooth sailing. Cody would definitely give her a rough ride.

Chapter Twelve

She managed to avoid Cody the following week although she couldn't help keeping an eye out for him, watching his comings and goings. He and Amy were constantly on the go.

That's why she found it odd that he hadn't even opened his drapes yet and it was already past noon. The Blazer was in the driveway and she could see the Harley through the open garage door. He was home, but he wasn't stirring.

She was just about to pick up the phone and check on him when it rang. She barely had a chance to answer before Cody's frantic voice came over the line.

"Something's wrong with Amy. Oh, no, Hallie, come quick!"

The alarm in his voice told her this wasn't one of his practical jokes or a lure to mess up her date. Besides, she didn't have a date. Tim was out of town at another of his bankers' conventions.

Racing through the house, Hallie grabbed a small medical case she kept with her on her meals-on-wheels deliveries—simple first aid and monitoring devices. She didn't know what was wrong with Amy, but wanted to be prepared.

Cody jerked the door open just as she mounted the steps, his little daughter flushed and listless in his arms.

"She's burning up," he said. "She's not coughing or crying like she's in pain or anything. She just lays here. And she's way too hot."

Hallie went into professional mode. She eased Amy from him and laid her on the couch, loosening the tapes on the disposable diapers.

Amy didn't even flinch when Hallie inserted a thermometer. As she waited for the temperature reading, she checked glands and reflexes. The glands were a little swollen, the reflexes nonresponsive. Her tiny bow lips were parched and cracked, a sign of dehydration. The thermometer read 104.6 degrees.

"What's wrong with her?" Cody demanded.

"I don't know, but this temp's nothing to mess with. I'll wrap her in warm towels to try to cool her off a bit—"

"Warm? Shouldn't we put her in cold water or something?"

"Normal body temperature is 98.6 degrees. Cold water will only shock her system. We need to take her in…" Before she could get the diaper retaped or finish her sentence, Amy went limp.

"Amy!" Hallie shouted, automatically checking for pulse and respirations.

Weak and shallow. Without warning Amy's tiny

body began to convulse. "Don't you do this to me, little girl!"

"Hallie, do something!"

"Dial 9-1-1. We need an ambulance." She snatched up the overheated child and ran to the bathroom, tossing towels into the tub, wrenching the taps at full force.

"Come on, baby. Hang in there. Easy does it." Oh, God, she wanted to scream, to cry, yet instincts had taken over, keeping her hands steady and confident.

She had the baby stripped and wrapped in sopping towels within seconds. She barely spared a glance for Cody who stood in the doorway with the diaper bag over his shoulder and keys in hand.

"Did you call for the ambulance?"

"It'll take too long. I can have us at the hospital in five minutes. Let's go."

"Cody..."

He urged her through the house, practically carrying both her and Amy. "You're trained, Hallie. I'd trust you with my life. Now I'm trusting you with my daughter's. Hurry."

Water from the wet towels dripped a path all the way to the car. Hallie was soaked and trembling and more scared than she'd ever been in her life. She'd dealt with emergencies plenty of times.

Never, though, when it was someone so close to her.

Someone she loved.

Hallie strapped herself into the Blazer and Cody

squealed out of the driveway, never letting up on the gas pedal.

"For heaven's sake, Cody. At least get us there in one piece."

Jaw clenched, he snatched up the car phone, punched in a remote number and spoke to the emergency room nurse, his voice clipped with barely leashed emotion. Hallie had a fleeting thought as to why he had the hospital's number stored in the phone's memory, but didn't voice the question. She didn't want to distract him.

He drove like a man possessed, his attention divided between the road and his baby daughter.

Hallie kept her finger on Amy's pulse. The baby no longer convulsed, but her coloring didn't look good.

Nor did her chest move.

She wasn't breathing!

Oh, please, Hallie prayed, moving the baby's head back, chin tilted. Tears streaked her cheeks as she fitted her mouth over those tiny blue lips, puffing shallow breaths of air into Amy's lungs.

Cody swore in a tone that bordered on panic. The Blazer came to a bone-jarring halt mere feet from the emergency room doors.

Hallie jumped out at a dead run and shouldered her way the swinging doors. She barely realized when professional hands snatched little Amy's limp body.

The ER erupted in a hive of activity, doctors shouting orders as nurses rattled off vitals and second-guessed instructions, hooking monitors, tubes and drips.

Hallie stood in the middle of it all, frozen in place, sopping towels clutched to her chest, her arms achingly empty without Amy's weight. Cold water dripped onto her feet, but she didn't notice. She stood at the bedside, wanting to help, but knowing she'd be no use in her condition.

Now that she wasn't the sole responsibility for the baby, she was in serious danger of falling apart. She'd seen distraught parents act this way countless times and recognized the emotion in herself.

She couldn't have loved little Amy more if the child had been born of her own womb. And she knew she needed to get a grip. She had to be strong.

Cody stood at her shoulder, still as stone, his pale blue eyes staring hard at each poke and prod of medical instruments. Fists clenched, the veins in his arms popped out like angry road maps. More than one nurse gave him wide berth. He looked like a man on the edge, a man about to lose it.

Michelle Beck moved to Hallie and took the wet towels from her. "Why don't you two wait outside? We'll call you when she's stabilized."

"I'm staying." Cody's voice was deadly quiet, yet held an air of command that brooked no argument. It would take a Marine tank to move him.

Hallie knew he was only hanging on to his emotions by a thread. She didn't want to push him over that thin line that held him together.

"We'll stay back out of the way, Michelle," she said softly, making an effort to steady her voice.

Michelle nodded, glanced at Cody, then moved back to the bedside where Amy lay. Hallie managed to coax Cody a few paces away. Familiar with the process, she watched monitors and listened to the progress reports uttered in rapid-fire. Fear still clawed at her chest even though Amy was now breathing on her own.

Hope surged through her veins as the activity in the ER became less frantic.

"She's stabilizing," Hallie whispered.

He still hadn't spoken. He just nodded and took a step toward the bed.

Hallie stopped him with a hand on his arm. "Cody. We need to stay out of the way."

"I've got to touch her. She needs to know that I'm here. She'll be scared."

His body was absolutely rigid. If it weren't for the raw emotion in his voice he would have appeared to be a robot.

Hallie understood his need to be near his daughter. And the familiar touch would be good for Amy. Patients rallied faster if they had a reason to fight. She stepped forward with him, her hand resting lightly at his shoulder, both for her own support as well as his.

Michelle moved aside to give Cody and Hallie room at the foot of the hospital bed.

The lump in Hallie's throat thickened as his large hand cupped Amy's tiny foot, his finger gently stroking the skin.

Cody's insides felt as if a grenade had just exploded in his path. He hated hospitals. The smell of sickness, medicine, death. The sounds of moans and tearful relatives.

They all looked the same, whether they were in Saint Thomas or Illinois.

Dennis had died in a hospital that had looked and felt very much like this one. Dennis. The best friend he'd ever had. And because the doctors had been unable to determine what was sucking away his vital life force, unable to save him, Cody had developed a mistrust of the medical profession.

He hated turning his baby daughter over to strangers, hated the chaos of the emergency room.

Hated the possibility of holding another person in his arms as they died.

"Excuse me, Mr. Brock?"

Cody barely glanced at the woman standing off to his side.

"Uh, we need your insurance information for Amy."

Damn it. He had insurance, but Amy wasn't listed as a dependent. He hadn't thought to do that. She was still so new to him.

"I'll be paying cash," he said tightly.

"We'd still like your insurance card."

God, these people were like vultures. Couldn't the woman see that now wasn't the time to be talking finances? "My daughter's not covered on my policy."

"Oh. I see. Well, if you could just fill out these forms and..."

Cody whirled around, more angry than he could remember being. He told the woman what she could do with her forms in blunt, graphic language, then snatched his wallet out of his hip pocket and slapped it in her hand.

"There's about eight hundred in cash and several credit cards with twenty-thousand-dollar limits, minimum. Will that get me through *today?*"

Hallie stepped in, easing his aggression with a gentle touch, and retrieved his wallet from the prune-faced ER paper pusher. She glanced at Cody, her brown eyes chastising his behavior. He ignored the reproach and turned back to his daughter.

"Give me the paperwork, Thelma," Hallie said. "I'll see that it gets filled out."

Cody winced as a nurse prepared another IV. He didn't think he could stand it. They were turning his baby into a human pin cushion.

"What's going on?" Cody asked the young ER doctor who was stripping latex gloves from his hands. "And talk to me in terms I can understand."

"The convulsions were brought on by the fever and dehydration. That's fairly common in babies when a fever spikes that way. We've got her stabilized and we're pumping antibiotics and fluids into her. That's about all I can tell you until we run tests. I'd like to admit her for a few days. We'll transfer her up to children's ICU, keep her comfortable, monitor her and see if we can't figure out what's going on. You can stay with her for a while if you like.''

"Just try and budge me," Cody muttered.

The doctor paused and grinned. "You *will* have to deal with those pesky forms sometime soon, though, so we can get her properly admitted.''

Cody glared and the doctor's grin widened, his palms held up in apparent surrender. "Don't shoot the messenger. I don't make the rules around here.''

Cody nodded and moved to Amy's side as the little girl whimpered and snuffled. It was such a pitiful, weak sound. He bent over the bed rail and leaned his forehead against his daughter's, noting that it was still warm, but not burning. He wanted to hold her, but she was attached to so much equipment, he didn't dare move her.

Her solemn, unblinking blue eyes stared up at him. He tried to imagine what went through her young mind. She seemed confused as to why he was allowing this to happen to her...seemed to say, "What's wrong? Why don't you fix it?''

Damn it, he felt like an utter failure. He didn't know *how* to fix it.

"It's going to be okay, baby. Daddy's here.'' He soothed her with words and gentle kisses, not even caring that his voice cracked.

He felt a gentle hand at his back, felt the brush of Hallie's breast as she slipped her arm around him. It gave him courage knowing he wasn't alone.

"They're ready to move her, Cody," she said softly. "We can ride up with her on the elevator, but then we'll have to wait while they get her settled in ICU.''

He stepped back as nurses went about disconnecting some of the wires. He reached out automatically, wanting to help as they transferred Amy onto a rolling stretcher.

''She'll be fine,'' Hallie soothed.

''What if she's not? Did I do something...or *not* do something that made her sick?''

''No, Cody. This isn't your fault. Babies just get sick sometimes.''

''Not to the point that they flop around like a fish and stop breathing. What if she has brain damage from lack of oxygen or something?''

''She didn't stop breathing for that long.'' Hallie didn't dare tell him the high fever might have done more damage than the lack of oxygen. ''We got her here in record time. That's the key to critical care. She'll be fine.''

''Thanks to you. Man, Slick, I don't know what I'd have done if you hadn't been there.''

''Handy thing having a nurse for a neighbor.''

His pale blue eyes narrowed, as if he were about to argue. All he said was, ''You're wet.'' He held out the keys to his Blazer. ''You need to go get into something dry. I don't think I could handle it if you got sick on me, too.''

Hallie glanced down at her shirtfront. The thin cotton clung to her bra like transparent plastic wrap. Her jeans weren't in much better shape. They looked as if somebody had tossed a bucket of water over her.

She made a mental note to retrieve Cody's towels before they left.

"Put your keys away. I'll just borrow a set of scrubs from the supply cabinet."

"Fine. How about that paperwork? Do you have the forms?"

"I've filled out most of them. I didn't know her birthday, or her full name, or...or her mother's name."

Cody's jaw clenched and Hallie was sorry she'd made mention of the other woman. He reached for his wallet and removed Amy's birth certificate and the lab results of her blood type.

"I forgot to put these away after I met with the attorney."

"So, you saw Derek?"

"Yeah. He'll try to locate Tanya, but said if he can't it's no big deal. Either way we can go to court and get physical custody legally recorded."

"We're ready to move Amy," Michelle said, interrupting them. "You can ride up with us if you want. Otherwise, Hallie knows the way."

Cody picked up Amy's little hand. "I'm going up. Hallie needs a change of clothes."

Michelle Beck raised a brow and grinned at Hallie. "Bossy, isn't he?"

"Yeah," Hallie agreed. "He forgets he's not a Marine sergeant anymore. Around here, his commands don't mean squat."

"Want to bet?" Cody said softly, dangerously. "If

you're not in dry clothes in the next ten minutes, I'll see to it myself.''

When Cody lowered his smooth voice that way every woman in the ER paused. For a split second, sound receded. Married or single, any female with a spark of hormones would react to that tone with vivid, private fantasies.

Hallie shivered. And it wasn't from the damp material sticking to her skin. She cleared her throat. "I'll meet you upstairs."

"Good girl."

Yes, by darn, she was a good girl. And it was pitiful that she was entertaining lurid fantasies of bad-girl behavior in the grave, somber setting of a hospital emergency room, standing at the bedside of a sick child.

THE PARKDALE GRAPEVINE worked with record speed. By the time Hallie had changed into drab green scrubs and made her way up to ICU, the waiting room was overflowing with concerned friends.

Hazel Crowley perched on the edge of her chair as George Delong paced. Miss Ida and Miss Lila, the retired schoolteachers bickered as usual. Pastor Collins started to intervene, then shook his head and joined Trina Lorry on the low gray couch.

Hallie wondered if Cody had taken the woman up on her offer of a home-cooked meal. At sixty, Trina mothered anyone who would let her and was the first to show up with a casserole or pot of soup when someone was in need.

Michelle, off duty now yet still in her nurse's uniform, moved around the room, explaining medical procedures.

Hallie felt her insides soften. What a great town. What great people. She'd taken their spirit for granted way too often.

If one of their flock had a need, they were right there, with food and support and prayers.

Leaving the crowd in Michelle's capable hands, Hallie waved to the desk nurse who buzzed her through a set of double doors leading to ICU.

Cody sat at Amy's bedside, his gaze shifting from the sleeping baby to the monitors hanging in the corner. He looked so out of place in the sterile surroundings, like a dark mercenary at a tea party, suspicious of everybody and everything. Each time one of the monitors beeped differently, his coiled body rose, his head whipping around as if he expected the whole staff to come running.

Hallie exchanged a knowing look with the ICU nurses and moved to his side.

"How's she doing?"

"How the hell should I know? These damned machines won't hold steady at any of the numbers. I don't know what any of it means. Alarms go off and all they do is push a reset button."

Hallie automatically picked up the chart at the end of the bed and studied it. Then she moved around and pointed to the different computerized lines on the monitor explaining what each number and graphic represented.

"All of this information is on a screen at the nurses' desk. They're monitoring it constantly. Amy's in good hands, Cody."

"I feel so helpless. I want her well."

"They've drawn blood and are running tests now. We should know something soon. In the meantime," she said, hoping to distract him, "have you seen the crowd in the waiting room?"

The corner of his mouth tipped up just a hint. "Yeah. They've come in one at a time. Except for the schoolteachers. They came in together...and got tossed out for bad behavior."

Hallie laughed softly. "That explains the squabbling I saw. I was surprised to even see them here, though."

Cody shrugged. "I ran into them the other day in town. They were having trouble with the Buick. I gave it a tune-up and they repaid me with dinner. I think the dinner invitation was only so they could spend more time with Amy."

He reached through the railing of the hospital crib and stroked his daughter's arm. "In a short period of time, she seems to have picked up several surrogate grandparents."

He glanced up at Hallie, his eyes tortured pools of blue.

"She's going to be all right isn't she, Slick?"

"Oh, Cody. Of course she is. The staff here is excellent. And Amy's a fighter."

"Dennis was a fighter," he murmured, lost in a memory that touched him too deep for tears. "He died in my arms. In a room that looked just like this. With wires and tubes and machinery beeping just like this.''

His voice was an agonized, rough whisper. Pain and compassion stung her heart and her eyes. She didn't even think about her actions, or worry over who might witness them. She simply slipped her arms around him. Since he occupied the only chair, she eased onto his lap, holding him, infusing him with every bit of strength she had to offer.

The thin surgical scrubs were no barrier against his heat. Firm thighs cradled her as his arms surrounded her, tightening, sharing the tragic loss of someone he had loved dearly. And sharing the worry over a tiny little girl with an unexplainable fever.

A nurse stepped into the curtained cubicle. Hallie started to rise, but Cody's arms tightened.

"Stay," he whispered. "Please. Just stay."

So she did. Sitting just that way for what seemed like endless hours, sharing his pain, his worry.

Telling herself any friend would do the same.

Admitting silently that she was the world's biggest liar.

ON THE SECOND NIGHT of their vigil, Hallie paused in the hospital room doorway, two paper cups of coffee in her hands.

Amy had been transferred to a private room. Cody sat in a rocking chair, holding his daughter, speaking softly. He hadn't shaved in two days and had barely taken time to eat. He'd slept in his clothes in a chair by Amy's bedside. The muted glow of an overhead lamp softened his weary, masculine features, as did the look of profound love as he gazed down at his baby girl.

Hallie just stood there, transfixed, and listened to his smooth, deep voice.

"Daddy's gonna buy you a dog. Would you like that, squirt? Every kid needs a dog. You need roots. I've got a lawyer who's making sure nobody can *ever* take you away from me."

The fierce emotion in his voice was enough to break her heart.

"It'll be a good life," he continued in a lighter tone. "You'll see. We'll play in the park and I'll let you ride on the back of my bike."

Hallie rolled her eyes at that. Hopefully he'd wait until she got a little bigger.

"And before you know it, you'll go to school and have dates." He stopped speaking, his dark brows drawing together in a frown. Hallie almost laughed when Amy's little forehead mimicked the action. She held her breath, though, because Cody hadn't realized she was standing there.

"I *know* I'm not ready for that," he said sternly. "No boys are gonna come around and mess with my little girl. No way. You see, boys are randy dudes. They've only got one thing on their minds."

"Speaking from personal experience, are we, Cody?" She figured she ought to put a stop to this detour in his storytelling. Cody's moods had run the complete range in the past two days, from volatile to

subdued and back again. He'd already lost his cool
once today, and it hadn't been a pretty sight.

He looked up and grinned. "Eavesdropping,
Slick?"

"Guilty as charged." She came through the doorway and set his cup on the tray by his side. "You
find out the juiciest stuff that way. Want me to spell
you for a while?"

He shook his head. "She's almost asleep. I'll just
rock her for a few minutes more."

Hallie perched a hip on the window sill, staring out
at the city lights. After a while, Cody rose and laid
Amy in the crib, then picked up his cup and joined
her at the window.

"I probably shouldn't have gotten you any more
caffeine," she said. "You're too wired as it is and
you need some rest."

"I'll rest when somebody gives me some firm answers," he said tightly.

"Has the doctor been back in?"

"No. He's a pathetic coward."

"Well, gee, Cody. It's a little nerve-racking to have
your life threatened."

"I didn't threaten his life."

"No? If somebody told me they intended to wring
my neck and squeeze a firm diagnosis out of me one
way or another, I might be inclined to question my
life expectancy."

"You're exaggerating."

"Am I?"

A muscle ticked in his jaw. "How can they not

know what caused Amy to be so sick? It's gross incompetence if you ask me. By damn, I'll have a cause if it takes a year to get it.''

"Sometimes these things just happen with kids and there's no medical explanation.''

"I'll get one.''

"Look at her, Cody. Her vitals are stable, color's good and the fever is gone. The white cell count is in the normal range, which means there's no sign of active infection. Everything is back to normal. Do you really want to put this child through needless pain and exhaustion for more tests when it's ninety-eight percent certain nothing will show up?''

"No. But what about the other two percent, Hallie? How can I rest easy without ever knowing what took my daughter so close to death?''

"Sometimes there are things that simply defy medical explanation. I've seen it before. I understand your torment, but there are times when you've just got to stand on faith.''

Man alive, she was beautiful, Cody thought. The setting was totally inappropriate for him to get caught up in her delicate features, but there was no help for it. It was damned tough to get past the shape of her lips, especially when she was so passionately wound up about a subject.

And now was not the time to tell Hallie to practice what she preached. If she'd take a chance, stand on faith like she advised him to do, they could stop all this push-pull stuff and get down to the business of having a relationship. A happy, *passionate* relationship.

She wanted to be his friend. He wanted more.

Needed more.

Michelle Beck breezed in and Cody's need remained unspoken.

"Okay, you two. I've been cleared to work this floor and I'm on for twelve hours. You guys need to go home and get some rest because the doc's probably going to spring Amy from our fine establishment in the morning."

Michelle pinned Cody with a no-nonsense look when he opened his mouth to argue.

"You look like hell, and that's putting it nicely, pretty boy. You won't be a bit of use to Amy if you're wiped out."

Pretty boy? He grinned despite himself. "You'd make a hell of a drill sergeant, Nurse Beck."

"Of course I would. And right now I'm sergeant of this room and I'm ordering you to go home. You too, Hallie."

Cody stood at military attention and saluted. Michelle smacked him on the arm and gave them both a shove.

"I'm trained to obey direct orders," he told Hallie. "Even if I don't agree."

"She makes sense, Cody. You can't take care of Amy if you fall asleep on your feet."

"Okay." He paused in the doorway, his blue eyes turning serious. "You've got my number?"

Michelle nodded.

"You'll call? Anytime. For anything. No matter how small?"

"I'll call you, Cody," Michelle said.

"Okay." But instead of leaving, he moved back into the room, gazing down at his sleeping daughter. He touched his fingers to his lips and gently transferred the imaginary kiss to Amy's Cupid's-bow mouth.

"Sleep tight, squirt," he whispered. "Daddy will only be five minutes away. And I'll be back first thing in the morning."

Hallie noticed that Michelle had ducked her head and was busily checking her pockets—probably for spare tissue. She didn't blame the nurse. Witnessing the private moment between Cody and his daughter would make a stone weep.

Chapter Thirteen

"What's wrong?"

Cody shut off the Blazer's idling engine and stared at his dark house. He didn't know if he could face going in there without Amy. He knew she was fine, that she'd be coming home in the morning. But until then, the hours would stretch endlessly.

"I haven't had Amy for long, but she's become so important to me." He rested his head against the leather seat and exhaled a weary breath. "Would it be okay if I came over to, uh…your house?"

He thought she was going to turn him down flat and he didn't know what he'd do. Silence stretched. Stars twinkled above the elm trees and crickets sang.

He turned his head, watching as she ran her palm nervously against the seam of her jeans. "I'm not asking you to sleep with me. I'm just not up to being alone right now."

She nodded, wisps of blond hair framing her face, brushing her shoulders. "Okay."

Cody hadn't realized he'd held his breath. Exhaling, he pulled the door handle and got out, following Hallie across the driveway to her house.

A Tiffany lamp cast a soft glow over the antique velvet sofa in the living room. With polished wood floors, fluffy throw pillows and happy sunflowers in every nook and cranny, the room practically begged him to kick off his shoes and stay awhile.

It was just the sort of surroundings Cody needed tonight.

"I appreciate you hanging around at the hospital these last couple of days."

"I wouldn't have wanted to be anyplace else. Cody, I'm just as crazy about Amy as you are."

"Yeah, but it took a bite out of your vacation time. And to spend it at the office so to speak. Well...thanks."

"You're welcome. Now sit before you fall. You're beat. Can I get you anything? I don't have any beer in the house, and I don't know about you, but I've had way too much coffee. How about hot chocolate?"

"I'm fine. And you're just as beat as I am. Why don't you sit down?"

She moved around the room, straightening things that didn't need straightening. A bundle of nerves, he noted, wondering about it.

"Uh, I think I'll change first. I feel as if I've slept in these clothes."

As Hallie disappeared down the hall, Cody wandered into the kitchen. She'd mentioned hot chocolate. He figured he could manage that. He really was exhausted. Tired to the bone. He'd been running on adrenaline the past few days, worried sick over his daughter.

He found a box of instant chocolate and reached in the cupboard for two mugs. His eyes fell on her damned chart. Laying there in plain sight. Right next to the microwave.

Hell, couldn't she even have the decency to hide the thing? The curiosity was more than he could stand.

He wanted to know if he was still on her list, even though she insisted vehemently that he wasn't. He'd been keeping his own mental tally of points in his favor. He figured they should be up there around the fifteen mark.

Sure enough, his name was still listed. But instead of the fifteen points he figured he deserved, his column total had a minus seven!

Damn it. Someone needed to set this woman straight. And he figured he was just the man to do it. He went back into the living room and sat on the couch, forgetting all about the hot chocolate.

When Hallie walked into the room, he glanced up—and felt as if his whole universe had ground to a halt.

She wore something soft, velour, he figured. The shapeless jogging suit should have made her look ordinary. Yet on Hallie, it looked spectacular. Her blond hair hung loose around her heart-shaped face, the ends flirting with the upper swells of her breasts.

His blood pumped with renewed vengeance, this time in desire instead of pique.

He held out a hand. "Sit with me?"

Her brown eyes turned wary. "Do you think that's wise?"

He nodded, his eyes never leaving her face. "Very wise."

"I thought you said—"

"I didn't ask you to strip, Slick. Just sit. Please?"

She sat. He eased his arms around her and tilted her chin up. This is exactly where she needed to be. Where he wanted her to be.

"Cody?"

"I lied. I *do* want you to strip. But I want to be the one to do it. I need you tonight, Hallie. I need your warmth—more than anything I've ever needed in my life."

He didn't give her a chance to voice a protest. He simply covered her lips with his.

Cody felt the beginnings of surrender shudder through her, felt her lips ease open on a low moan. He'd kissed her in need, a need to erase the terror of the past two days, days where the life of his small daughter hung in the balance. And a need to prove to her that intimacy between them was right.

Need became so much more, though, with the warmth of her mouth pressed against his, the sway of her body as she eased closer.

He'd known desire before. He appreciated women, all their intricate facets, their smell, their walk, their subtle games.

But he'd never felt so intoxicated by one, so stunned by a touch that he shook with it. He pulled her tighter to him, fisting his hand in the silk of her blond hair. Something urgent and primitive came over him, consumed him as he gripped her hips and jerked her beneath him on the couch. He wanted this woman bound to him, wanted her so filled with him there would never be any room for doubt. Or another man.

Hallie sucked in a sharp breath, stunned by his aggression...thrilled by it. Her heart pounded and she felt dizzy. He clamped her wrists together in one powerful hand, jerking her arms above her head.

As if he expected her to vanish.

She couldn't have left him at that moment if her very life depended on it. "Cody?"

His blue eyes were fierce with an emotion she couldn't define. He looked at her for a charged instant, as if he couldn't understand why she'd interrupted him.

Then the expression cleared and his grip eased. "Oh, man, Slick. Did I hurt you?"

"No." Her hands cupped his face, her thumbs smoothing over his prominent cheekbones, his jaw, soothing him. A two-day stubble rasped beneath her wandering fingers. "I'm not going anywhere," she whispered.

"Promise?"

"For now." Their eyes locked and held. Hallie pressed a fingertip to his lips when he would have spoken. "No more words, Cody. No questions. Just give me right now. Make love to me."

And he did, taking her on a journey of gentle

touches and whispered murmurings. Just murmurings, though. No words, as she'd asked.

He spoke to her with his hands and his mouth and his eyes. He made her burn, from her toes to her scalp. Every place his palm skimmed or his fingers lingered left her singed and aching for more.

Her own hands became restless, fevered, desperate to give back a measure of the pleasure that hummed through her veins like hot mercury, desperate to feel all of him against her.

Impatient, she jerked at his shirt, pulling it from the waist of his jeans. Lips clung and breaths mingled as he shrugged out of his shirt. Their hands tangled in a frantic attempt to undress each other. He swore against her lips, her throat, her breasts, his chest heaving as he finally got her jeans all the way off.

And that's when Cody lost all shred of control. The scent of lavender surrounded him, wafting up from the heat of her skin. He tasted the scent on his tongue, tasted the passion that hung heavy in the air.

She was pure, erotic sin, avid in her participation, sending him over the edge of madness. Her fingertips brushed his manhood and he nearly exploded.

She strained against him, demanding, and he gave before she could even ask, much more than either one of them might have anticipated.

It was all heat and ache and sweet ecstasy. His fingers dipped into her, sending her soaring. Like fire to dry tender, she ignited in his arms, sparking an answering inferno in him.

He plunged inside her, a madness so sweet, so

powerful, it consumed him, wiping away all reason. This is where he wanted to be. Where he needed to be. Especially tonight. Especially after the ordeal with Amy. He needed to lose himself in Hallie, to reaffirm that there was power and passion and vital life force.

Her fingers dug hard into his shoulders as she arched to meet his thrusts. He wanted the feeling to last forever, knew he was lost when he felt her shudder around him, fly apart in his arms. He buried his face in her hair as his own release crashed through him, sending him straight off the razor's edge of sanity.

SOMEHOW, THEY'D ENDED UP on the floor, cushioned only by the oriental rug with its raised cabbage roses. Standing on either side of the fireplace hearth were two wooden sunflower dolls, their smiling, freckled faces with round painted eyes appearing to watch the human activity with innocent glee. Hallie might have laughed at the fanciful thought if she'd had the energy—or the breath.

She felt as if someone had drugged her. Pleasurably.

"I meant to be gentle with you," Cody murmured against her neck. He shifted his weight to his side. "You okay?"

"Mmm," was all she could manage. Cody had been like a wild, unstoppable, sensual force tonight. She understood the emotions, the frenzy, the loss of control. Especially after these last few days at the hospital with Amy.

As a nurse, Hallie had watched the behavior and reactions of parents of sick kids. Once, a young mother had confided—with a fair amount of guilt—that she'd made wild love to her husband as a means of releasing her emotions after her child was on the mend.

So Hallie understood what had just happened between her and Cody. Tonight had been for healing, for celebration. Next time, she thought lazily, would be for gentleness.

His fingertip whispered along the sensitive underside of her breast and she found she did have breath left after all. A quiet, helpless gasp escaped her.

"I always knew you'd be like this," he said, his finger tracing lower, causing her stomach to dip. "I've dreamed about it for years."

She was so quiet, her touch featherlight as she outlined the tattoo on his arm.

"How long have you had this?"

"I got it after Dennis died."

"The two hands clasped in friendship," she said softly. "That's nice. And *SemperFi?* What does it mean?"

"It's from Latin—*semper fidelis*. Means 'always faithful.'" To the Marines, and to Dennis.

And to Hallie if she'd give him a chance.

He stood and lifted her.

"What are you doing?" She grabbed his shoulders for balance, her skin furnace hot.

"I'm taking you to bed. This time we're going to go slow if it kills me."

"Cody…"

"Shh." He pressed his lips against hers, the best way he knew how to silence her, to buy himself more time. He'd almost lost his daughter. He didn't want to lose Hallie, too. And he knew if he gave that smart, logical, good-girl mind of hers time, she'd more than likely make an excuse to stop him.

And tonight, he didn't want to be stopped. He wanted her surrender. Wanted to show her all the desire and satisfaction he had in him to give.

Because with Hallie, their hearts spoke so much better than words.

It took nearly all of Cody's willpower to leave Hallie's bed and get dressed the next morning. But Amy would be waking soon and he didn't want her left alone in that hospital room any longer than necessary.

He made coffee and brought a cup to Hallie. She was just shrugging into her robe.

"Are you going with me to pick up Amy?"

She shook her head and wouldn't meet his eyes. "I really need to get some things done around here. I'll come see her when you get home."

He felt her withdrawal like a tug to his heart. He wanted to stay and demand that she face what they had together, but Amy was waiting. He'd let her get away with it. For now.

"Okay. I'll call you."

She nodded and did look at him then. What he saw

in her sleepy brown eyes rocked him to his toes. He saw both love and resignation.

A love that was bittersweet and a resignation that told him she meant to tell him goodbye.

He wasn't sure if he deserved the love. He knew he didn't deserve the goodbye.

"I'll call you," he repeated, wings of panic making his voice harsh. "We need to talk."

Before she could argue with him, Cody turned and left, letting himself out the front door.

Caught up in the frightening thought of Hallie being in love with him, he nearly tripped over the woman sitting on his front doorstep.

He didn't know which emotion to give in to. He was at once stunned, angry and deadly calm.

He settled for the deadly calm.

"Tanya. What brings you here?"

"My daughter."

He raised a brow. "It's a little late to be thinking about her now, isn't it?"

"I've got a life, you know," she defended.

"Yeah. Well, why don't you get back to it. Amy's doing just fine without you." He knew he shouldn't have challenged her like that. He saw her heavily made up blue eyes narrow.

"I'm surprised at you, Cody. You don't strike me as the fatherly type. And she's my daughter."

"Mine, too," he reminded, using all of his control not to shout. "I was presented with a set of blood tests to prove it. As to your surprise at my fatherly abilities, I'm damned good at it."

"You're not finding that it cramps your social life being a single parent? I couldn't help but notice that you're just getting home. Where is our little Amy by the way?"

Panic clutched him like a vise but he kept his expression stoic. Tanya would pick at a weakness like a vulture. He couldn't believe he'd ever gotten *that* drunk!

On the heels of that thought came another. One that jolted him like a California earthquake. There had been only one time in his life when he'd neglected to use protection. The consequence had been Amy.

Now, he realized, there was a second. With Hallie. Last night. He'd dropped his guard.

Not because he was drunk.

But because he loved her!

Hell of a time to get such an insight, Brock.

Tanya was still staring at him, her dark lashes thick with mascara. He didn't intend to tell her that Amy was in the hospital. He wouldn't put it past her to use her theatrical training to rush over there, acting the concerned parent when she wasn't that at all.

Not by any stretch of the imagination.

"You gave up your rights to Amy the day you walked out on her."

"No, I didn't! I left her in capable hands. With my parents."

"Parents on a social security income and in poor health. Do you have any idea how much money and energy go into taking care of an eleven-month-old child?"

"Don't pull that crap on me, Cody. I'm the one who suffered through sixteen hours of labor with that kid and struggled to make ends meet."

"I would have paid child support, Tanya. You didn't have to abandon her like she was yesterday's bathwater."

She rolled her eyes. "Look. I didn't come here to argue. I came to take the kid off your hands."

The kid. She was a piece of work. She reminded him too damned much of someone else. His own mother, to be exact.

"Too bad. As it happens, I don't want *Amy* taken off my hands." He stressed his daughter's name deliberately. Disgusted, he realized it had gone right over Tanya's head.

"You're trespassing, Tanya, and I've got someplace to be. If you've got anything else to say to me, here's my attorney's number." He withdrew Derek's card from his wallet and slapped it in her hand. Then he went into the house and shut the door, leaning against it, his heart thundering in his chest.

What now? Amy was waiting for him, but he didn't want Tanya following him to the hospital.

He snatched up the phone and punched out Derek's private number.

The attorney answered on the second ring.

"Evidently you must have located Tanya," Cody said.

"I put an investigator on it, yes. It'd be a lot easier if we could get her to sign an amicable custody agreement."

"I don't think she intends to be amicable. She showed up here this morning. In her words, to take *the kid* off my hands."

"This moves things up a bit. It's too bad you're not married. It'd be easier to prove suitability of environment and stability."

Hallie's image flashed in his mind. Maybe he could do something about his marital status.

"Tanya could show her true colors and skip out of town as fast as she skipped into it. If she doesn't, how soon can we get to court?"

"I'll check with the judge today. It could be as early as tomorrow, or it could be a month. Depends on the cases pending."

"Do what you have to do, Engle. And do it quick. I'm *not* losing my daughter."

THE MORE CODY thought about the idea, the more right it felt. Now all he had to do was lay his heart on the line and hope Hallie would agree, hope he hadn't read the message in her eyes wrong. He dumped the diaper bag on the sofa, set the hospital discharge papers on the coffee table, kissed Amy's forehead for luck, then picked up the telephone.

"Hey, Slick," he said when she answered the phone. "Amy's asking for you."

"Is that so?"

"Yeah." He grinned and jiggled his daughter in his arm. "Said she wanted to see 'Sick.'"

"That little stinker. Put her on the phone."

"Uh-uh. She want's you to come over."

There were several beats of silence on the phone and Cody's palms began to sweat. Then he heard her sigh.

"Okay. I'll be there in a few minutes."

Cody hung up the phone and gave Amy a loud smacking kiss on her cheek. "She won't be able to resist either of us," he told his daughter.

HALLIE HELD AMY in her lap. The child was back to her old self. Babies rallied so quickly. "You'd never know she was so sick," she said, burying her lips in Amy's hair. "But you're way too rambunctious. How about if I rock you for a few minutes? Want to go night-night?"

Amy shook her head, sending jet-black curls swinging, yet her eyelids were drooping.

"Okay," Hallie agreed. "No night-night. We'll just rock."

Cody leaned a shoulder against the jamb, watching the scene from the kitchen doorway. Hallie was so good with his daughter. Amy had a thumb stuck in her mouth, her other hand was wound in Hallie's silky platinum hair.

In no time at all, Amy was fast asleep. Hallie looked up and caught his stare. She smiled and rose to lay the baby down.

When she came back in the room, she hesitated and looked at the front door.

"We need to talk," Cody said.

"About what?"

"Us."

She shook her head.

Panic swamped him, making him feel as if he were treading in quicksand. "I need a wife," he blurted.

Her brown eyes widened. "Excuse me?"

Cody raked a hand through his hair. "That wasn't very smooth. It's just that I'm such a wreck right now. Tanya's back."

"Amy's mother?"

"Yes. If you could call her that. You've been more of a mother to that little girl than Tanya ever was."

"Is she going to fight you for custody?"

"Looks that way. Listen, Slick, I didn't plan to ask you this way. You deserve flowers and champagne and soft lighting. But I didn't expect Tanya to show up. Derek says it would look better in the court's eyes if I were married."

Need, Hallie thought. Not love.

Only an all-consuming passion that frightened her down to her toes.

She shook her head and backed toward the door.

Cody snagged her before she'd taken two steps. "What is it? We're good together, Hallie. We were meant to be."

She just kept shaking her head. Now Cody felt as if he were swimming in a pool of alligators, which were snapping at him with hungry jaws. Painful jaws.

"Damn it, Hallie. When will you say it?"

"What?"

"That you love me?"

This time her blond hair swung across her shoulders with the force of her head movement. She wasn't denying anything, but neither was she admitting.

He stepped close, crowding her, cupping her cheek in his palm. "Marry me, Hallie."

"I can't."

"Yes, you can. We're good together, Slick. You're not the only one frightened by a dream, by life. Stay with me. Marry me. Let me touch that part of you deep inside. You know you want me to. I know it's in your heart to stay."

Time stood still in silence. Her eyes brimmed with tears. His thumb caught a salty drop. The pain and denial in her brown eyes was like acid singeing his soul.

Desperate, he grasped for a lifeline. "What if you're pregnant?"

"I'm on the Pill."

Figures. He was losing ground by the second.

"How can you stand there and deny the fire between us?" He knew he'd made a big mistake the minute he said the words. He saw it in the rise of her chin, in the set of her shoulders.

"Fire burns, Cody. And it eventually goes out, leaving behind cold, bitter ashes." She knew that better than most. She'd lived it. She'd never want to put Cody's little girl, or any future children they might have, through that torment. She needed safe, tidy emotions.

"Not always," he argued.

Hallie felt as if her heart were being ripped out. She heard the tinkle of bells and her insides lurched.

He wasn't her destiny. She'd almost given in. Almost forgotten the lesson that had been branded into her over a lifetime. The mystical warning might be a figment of her imagination, or it truly might be Sabrina, watching over her shoulder, keeping her on the right track, reminding that the heart can make mistakes, but the head was what she should listen to.

But what if she was wrong? What if Cody *was* her destiny?

No! Those were only foolish thoughts. Foolish emotions.

She'd taken a detour in life, a side journey for pleasure. Now she had to seek her true destiny. The destiny that had been foretold so many years ago.

With a safe man. A man who would give her an easy life.

Passion is at the root of your problem. She'd been reminded of that more than once. And Cody Brock was a man who could have invented passion.

"I'm sorry, Cody."

Cody was without words. Here he stood with his heart in his hands and she'd rejected him. His whole world had gone wrong and he didn't know what to do, didn't know how to convince her she could trust him with her heart.

That damned scorecard, he thought. He wanted to storm over to her house, find the evil thing and burn it.

Instead, he just stood there and watched her walk away.

The woman he'd loved since childhood.

More than anything, Cody wanted love. And he wanted a family.

His love had just walked out on him.

And depending on the mercy of an impartial judge who knew nothing about him, he stood to lose his family, too.

A viselike pain gripped his heart and squeezed. It was an ache he hadn't experienced since his real mother had fessed up to her deception, snatching away his foundation, making him realize his life up to that point had been based on a lie.

Was he a fool to believe he had anything that Hallie needed? That he was good enough? Was he still the bad boy with a chip on his shoulder? A guy who'd dealt his parents so much misery?

Miranda and Gerald were no longer here to offer comfort or answers. But there was one person who could tell him.

He called Hazel to sit with Amy. He needed the wind in his face right now. Needed the speed and danger of the Harley.

Because right now he felt dangerous.

"MIZ FITZPATRICK?" Cody called through the doorway.

"Come in, Cody."

He moved into the tiny living room, spotting Edna Fitzpatrick sitting in her usual chair, a crochet needle in her frail hands, a half-completed afghan resting in her lap.

"How'd you know it was me?"

She laughed softly. "I might be blind, but my hearing's perfectly fine. Only one boy I remember who roars around on a death trap motorbike." She laid her crocheting aside and patted the ottoman in front of her. "Come sit and we'll talk. I've been expecting this visit."

Cody obeyed her directive, and took the hands she held out to him. Old hands. Gentle hands. Hands so like his mother's. No, he corrected. Not his mother's. His grandmother's.

"How are you feeling?" he asked, suddenly very unsure of his purpose for being here. He didn't even know how to broach the subject.

"I'm an old woman without eyesight, but I feel great. Which is more than I can say for you. There's no call to be so troubled, Cody."

He shook his head. "I made my parents' life miserable. They gave up the best years of their lives for me, and I went out of my way to give them grief. They're gone now and I don't know how to make it up to them. To say I'm sorry."

Her wrinkled brow drew together, then her lips parted as if in discovery. "Oh, you sweet boy. You're feeling guilty. But I tell you, it's misplaced. Miranda loved you. She was so proud of you!"

It was what he'd hoped. What he needed to hear. "Are you sure? I didn't keep in touch like I should have over the years. I had it in the back of my mind to come back after I'd made something of myself. I wasted a lot of years. And then it was too late."

"No. It wasn't too late. Don't you buy into that

garbage of not being good enough. Miranda understood your hurt. And she carried around her own guilt for not telling you, for having that sister of yours blurt out the truth the way she did. Of course Miranda worried over the rough crowd you got mixed up with, but she never doubted that you'd make the right decisions."

"She accused me of making messes and not taking responsibility." Those words had been what pushed him to enlist in the Marines.

"And she regretted those words. She once said that she didn't know how to love you enough to ease your suffering. That you were so afraid of more pain and rejection, you created it yourself so you could meet it on your own turf."

"Yeah. I suppose I did live by the motto of Do Unto Others Before They Have A Chance To Do Unto You."

"Every teenager rebels, honey. You had more reason than most. But you turned into a fine man. Miranda was proud of that. Proud that she'd had a hand in shaping you."

"Thank you," Cody said.

"Now, tell me what's going on with you and our sweet Hallie Fortune."

"That's another mess. A roadblock I can't seem to get past." He found himself relating the whole story to the old woman.

"Cody, you came here wanting reassurance that your parents loved you, that they knew you loved them. Now you just think about that for a minute."

"You lost me."

"Everybody needs the words. Have you said them to Hallie? Have you told that sweet girl how much you love her?"

"Yes." *No.* Cody nearly slapped his forehead. He swore, then apologized for doing so in front of Edna.

She excused his lapse with a delighted laugh. "No need to apologize to me. My Raymond was a man known to curse a blue streak—quite elegantly, I might add. And he was stingy with love words. Oh, he felt them. Passionately. He just forgot to send them from the brain to the mouth. Are you drawing any gender parallels here?"

Cody laughed. "Yeah. I am." He leaned forward and placed a soft kiss on her wrinkled cheek. "Thanks, Miz Fitzpatrick. Mom was lucky to have you for a friend. And so am I."

"I'VE GOT A TELEGRAM for Hallie Fortune."

"I'm Hallie Fortune."

The delivery boy with a Western Union logo over his pocket held out an envelope and a clipboard. "Can you sign here for me?"

Hallie signed her name, her hands trembling. Who would send her a telegram? On TV, telegrams usually meant bad news.

She ripped open the envelope, her eyes skipping right to the signature. Maggie.

Getting married. Stop. *Name's J. D. MacIntyre, a hell of a cowboy.* Stop. *Will explain all when I see you.* Stop. *Clarissa's married her millionaire.* Stop. *What's up with the guy next door?* Stop.

Hallie sank onto the couch, dazed, butterflies dancing in her stomach.

Who had Clarissa married? The oilman from Oklahoma? It had only been a matter of weeks since she'd gone to Tiffany's with Clarissa—and accused her of choosing more jewelry than the Queen owned.

There had been a frantic, desperate feel to the outing, but Hallie had kept most of her thoughts to herself. Clarissa deserved happiness. She'd gone without for way too long.

Hallie fingered the telegram, feeling thoroughly disoriented. It was just like Maggie to do something impulsive like this—and not give sufficient details! She laughed and hugged the telegram to her chest.

"Ooo-rah, Maggie and Clarissa," she whispered, unconsciously using Cody's Marine phrase.

The magic had worked.

But not for her.

Destiny, Maggie had said. *Grab it with both hands and run with it.*

Both Clarissa and Maggie had done that—chosen their destiny and set about to make it happen. It was time for Hallie to do the same.

Chapter Fourteen

Hallie dressed with care in a black skirt and khaki-colored belted trench jacket. The skirt was short and sexy, made even more so by the high-heeled pumps on her feet, but the jacket lent an air of respectability.

Respectability that was expected of a banker's wife.

She told herself not to think of Cody as she drove into town—as she passed the courthouse.

Her heart lurched. His Blazer was in the parking lot of the court building.

Destiny, she reminded herself, suppressing the urge to hang a quick left instead of going the extra block to the bank. First things first, she told herself. After she settled things with Tim, she'd stop by the courthouse, just in case Cody needed a character witness.

She parked around the side of the bank, intending to use the side entrance closest to Tim's office. Her heels clicked across the cement echoing the thud of her heart.

Surely she was doing the right thing.

From the corner of her eye, she caught movement by Tim's white sedan. And heard raised voices.

Tim's raised voice.

She stopped, frowning. Tim never raised his voice. He was the most easygoing, nonargumentative man she'd ever known.

Yet contrary to that image, his hands gripped Crissy Metz's shoulders and his voice carried loud enough for the patrons inside the bank building to hear. Good grief, she'd never seen Tim act this way. Aggressive. Hot.

Her mind flashed back to her birthday celebration. Tim had been arguing with Crissy then.

"Damn it, Crissy!" he shouted. "I love you! And I won't let you put me off with any more of this class distinction stuff!"

Before Hallie's stunned eyes, Tim hauled Crissy to him and kissed her. It was a kiss that burned.

A kiss that Hallie recognized because she'd been the recipient of quite a few just like it.

From Cody.

She must have made a noise because Crissy's eyes suddenly popped open, staring straight at Hallie. Distress fairly shouted as Crissy pushed against Tim's shoulder, finally getting his attention.

When he turned, a fiery intensity burned in his eyes, an intensity that had never been present with her.

It was the same emotion that burned in Cody's eyes when they were together.

Cody did love her! How could she have been so blind?

Sabrina must have made a mistake. No, Hallie thought. *She'd* been the stubborn one.

She should have known. His heart spoke to her without words, his smile held her. The gentle touch of his hand had always been there to catch her when she fell. He brought her sunflowers and made love to her with passion, yet with soul-deep feelings.

Hallie had latched on to a belief and allowed it to blind her. A lot of relationships had passion and they didn't all end up like her parents'. The key was true love. It was what she felt for Cody.

Discomfort and embarrassment hung heavy in the air as Tim and Crissy and Hallie stared at one another. Hallie sliced right through it by grinning. "Bad timing on my part. You two carry on."

"Hallie," Tim said, "I'm sorry you found out this way. You're what I thought I wanted—the perfect image of a banker's wife. I was wrong, though. It's Crissy that I love. The image doesn't mean a damn." This last was said as much for Crissy's benefit as for Hallie's.

And, she realized, she'd been operating on the same misguided belief. Both she and Tim had sought an image rather than love. Tim had been her image of the perfect boy next door. She had been his idea of the perfect banker's wife.

Looking at Tim, his arm possessively around Crissy, Hallie didn't feel the least bit betrayed. She felt relieved. "There were no bankers' conventions, were there?'' The question was voiced without accusation. Just simple curiosity.

Tim shook his head. Crissy looked stricken. Any guilt Hallie had harbored vanished and she laughed.

They'd *both* been two-timing on the same day!

"You're not mad?" Crissy asked.

"No," Hallie said. And she truly wasn't. Tim might have the right qualifications on her scorecard, but she didn't love him.

"I'm sorry," Tim said again. "Jeez, this is awkward."

"It shouldn't be. Just out of curiosity, though…" She didn't know how to ask this question without sounding like a rejection case. "What was it about us that…" Hell, this wasn't going well at all. "Forget it."

"Passion," Tim said.

Hallie jolted. That damned word was beginning to be both her bane and her salvation.

"You're more like a sister to me, Hal. But Crissy and I have passion."

Yes. And so did she, Hallie thought. And her passion was facing a courtroom by himself. Fighting for the right to keep his baby daughter.

And she'd abandoned him.

Just like she'd feared he'd do to her.

She was an idiot! True love did not fail. It even said so in the Bible!

She rushed up to Tim, kissed him square on the lips, then turned and did the same to a startled Crissy.

"Thank you, both! Have a wonderful life—and don't forget to invite me to the wedding!"

She cursed her high heels as she sprinted back to her car. She was on a mission—the *right* mission this time.

There was a bad boy and a baby who needed her.

So what if he'd never said anything about love. She was more than willing to point out the error of his ways.

HALLIE SLIPPED IN through the back doors of the courtroom. She needn't have practiced stealth. It was a madhouse.

Lila and Ida were front and center, glaring at the judge whose face had turned an unbecoming shade of red. Hallie had a concern for his blood pressure reading.

"Smart as a whip that boy was," Ida said, shoving her spectacles back up on her nose. "Taught him myself in sophomore English. Sister, here," she nodded toward Lila, "had him in the senior year. Hardly ever needed to study, which was a good thing since he had a pesky habit of being truant." Her eyes widened, apparently realizing how her words might have been taken. "Oh, but truancy's not so bad. And half the time it was those wicked girls' fault you know. Why, they ran after him something fierce. And you know how impressionable young boys can be. It's understandable he'd skip class a time or two."

Cody groaned.

Judge Atherton's bushy gray eyebrows lowered.

"For the benefit of the young people in the court-room, let's not be advocating truancy."

Lila piped up, then. "Ida, you're making a don-key's hind end out of yourself and hurting Cody Brock's case. Why don't you just step down and let me do the talking!"

The spectators in the courtroom tittered. Judge Atherton appeared to be biting his lip to keep from laughing. Derek Engle propped his arm on the back of Cody's chair, not making a single objection.

Cody groaned again and pinched the bridge of his nose. Amy, sitting in George Delong's lap shrieked with laughter, obviously deciding she'd missed some-thing crucial and would have none of it.

Every soul in the courtroom responded to the child's laughter with sweet smiles and nods of ap-proval.

"See there," Lila added, determined to get her two cents' worth in even if Ida had the official floor. "That's a happy child. It'd be a crying shame to rip her from her daddy's arms. Cody Brock is em-ployed—have you seen that sweet comic strip he draws? I tell you he's the perfect Mr. Mom. He works at home where he can give that little girl all the at-tention and love she needs." Lila nodded firmly. "Case closed!"

"Thank you," the judge said dryly, "for rendering my decision."

"Any fool could see what the decision should be." Lila sniffed, and tugged at the hem of her navy blouse.

"My decision should be to find *you* in contempt of court, madam!"

"Now wait just a doggone minute Henry Atherton," Ida admonished in her best schoolteacher tone. "That's my sister you're threatening!" The courtroom erupted with several people talking at once. The judge banged his gavel to no avail.

Hallie could only catch bits and snatches of what was said. She shook her head. It seemed like the whole town had turned out to champion Cody and his baby daughter. Hallie also noted that the other party—Amy's mother—was missing. Hadn't the woman cared enough to even show up at court?

That in itself should weigh heavily in Cody's favor.

Hallie heard the courtroom doors open and glanced over her shoulder, wondering who had come to join the circus.

In walked Clarissa and Maggie—each had a gorgeous man by their side. Both women grinned and pointed to their escorts as if to say, "Check this out."

Hallie jumped up from her seat in the back row, hugging her cousin and best friend, then stepped back.

She studied Maggie and the man beside her. "J.D., I presume?"

Maggie's sky blue eyes danced with amusement. "You got it in one, 'cuz. We came to personally invite you to the wedding." They made a striking couple—Maggie, six feet of gorgeous curves, honey blond hair and model perfect features, her J.D. topping out at a good six foot six. A sexy, *tall* Tom

Selleck look-alike, he gazed at his bride-to-be with a look of indulgence and profound love.

Hallie turned to Clarissa, her brow raised. "He doesn't look anything like the Oklahoma oilman."

Clarissa's smile beamed. "Hallie, meet my husband, Conor James."

Hallie heard the musical tinkle of bracelets and looked past her friends.

Sabrina appeared in the doorway, resplendent in magenta satin.

She remembered the conversation with Maggie, remembered the mystical wagon that had appeared as if it were a hallucination. Her curiosity was too strong to hold back.

"Sabrina. How did you know? How could you be in three places on the same day?" Although Hallie had been the most doubtful of the three women, Clarissa and Maggie also waited avidly for the answer.

Sabrina's bracelets tinkled again as she waved a dismissive hand, her smile holding an eternity of secrets. "We all make our own destiny, sweet Hallie."

"But…"

"Ah, you must realize that an illusionist *never* reveals her methods."

Maggie was the first one to nod, to accept without question. "I've got my cowboy," she said.

"And I, my millionaire," Clarissa added, snuggling up to Conor with a look so bright with love any fool could see she'd have married him even if he didn't have a dime to his name.

"And," Maggie injected, "if I'm not mistaken, that's Cody Brock looking at you as if the sun rises and sets just for you—your boy next door."

Slowly, Hallie turned. Sure enough, Cody's attention was focused on her. Their gazes met and clung, like a special brand of magic.

The crowd murmured, then became hushed. The judge, looking resigned for more interruptions picked up his gavel, then laid it aside with a weary sigh and folded his hands.

"Now why couldn't *I* accomplish that?" Atherton asked rhetorically. Apparently needing to get a last word in before he lost the crowd's attention completely—although he already had—Atherton cleared his throat.

"Mr. Brock?"

Cody turned, reluctantly, it seemed. "Yes, sir?"

"Since the child's mother has already left town and has agreed by signature that she will not contest your petition, this court awards full legal and physical custody of Amelia Dawn Brock to you."

A slow grin creased Cody's cheeks. "Thank you, sir."

"Have your attorney finalize the documents and I'll sign them. In the meantime, in the interest of love—which I suspect is at the root of this uncanny disruption of these proceedings...do carry on."

"Thank you, sir. I intend to."

Cody turned, his laser blue eyes pinning Hallie right where she stood.

It seemed that no one took a breath. Absolute silence reigned as all eyes darted from Cody to Hallie.

"Woman," Cody said, his low, hushed voice bouncing off the walls of the courtroom like a ricochet bullet. "You take my breath away."

"Oh!" Maggie and Clarissa sighed in unison.

Hallie never took her eyes from Cody. She felt three hands at her back.

Maggie's, Clarissa's and Sabrina's.

"Choose passion, my sweet," Sabrina advised. "Believe in the magic of love. It is time to complete the circle."

"Go for it," Maggie whispered.

"You deserve happiness," Clarissa added softly.

Cody took the first steps, intent evident in each stride. The sexy grin on his face made her knees week. The bad-boy swagger so reminiscent of the old days sent her heart skipping double time.

Hallie didn't even realize her own feet were moving. It was as if love's gravity were pulling her to his side, where she should always be.

Without pausing, he swept her into his arms and lowered his head, hauling her into an earthshaking kiss that nearly set her on fire.

She had trouble drawing a breath when at last he raised his head.

"I'm your man, Hallie Fortune. I'm not nice and easy like those other guys you've been dating. I can't promise that we won't fight, but I can promise you we'll never do it in front of the kids. And we'll have a hell of a time making up afterward."

"Cody!" She felt her face flame, felt a bubble of laughter well up.

"Lighten up, Slick. There's a bad girl lurking just below the surface of that prim Goody Two-shoes facade you show the rest of the world, so your argument about my shady character won't cut it. Just ask Edna Fitzpatrick."

"Absolutely," Edna said from the side of the courtroom. "I'll vouch for the boy."

Cody grinned, but his eyes never left Hallie's. Hallie in turn, was almost too stunned to speak. My God, they were in the middle of a courtroom with half the town looking on. And Cody had her held up against him so tightly, it would have taken the jaws of life to pull them apart.

"You say that commitment's not my thing, but I'm here to tell you it is. I happen to love you, lady."

Hallie nearly swooned. She opened her mouth, intending to take issue with the fact that he'd never said anything about love before now, but his lips once again descended, forcing the words back down her throat.

"I don't *need* you to take care of my daughter, but I *want* you to. Marry me, Slick. Be my wife. Amy's mom. Look around you."

His hand swept the room in a all-encompassing gesture. Hallie could have told him at this point that further argument wasn't necessary, but frankly she was pleased with Cody's show of affection and declaration in public. She wanted to see how far he'd go with it.

"I'll bet there are folks here who've been happily married for forty years or more."

Several men and women in the avid audience raised their hands. Just about everyone present had an encouraging comment to toss out at Hallie.

"I've found a home here, Slick, in a place where I didn't think I'd be accepted. Edna pointed out that my guilt was misplaced and that I'm remembering events through the eyes of a teenage rebel. I'm a father now, a changed man. I took a chance and so can you."

His fingers tunneled through her hair. "Do you love me?"

At last Hallie had the opportunity to speak. "You're worse than Lila and Ida as far as letting somebody get a word in edgewise, Cody Brock. Of course I love you."

He looked as if he were about to lose his composure. "You do?"

"Absolutely. I've loved you since I was a girl of twelve. I came here today to make sure you wouldn't lose Amy. And to point out to you, in no uncertain terms, that you love me."

His smile was tender, his gaze steady. "I forgot to give you the words, didn't I?"

"Yes. A minor detail." She ran her palm over his muscled arm where his tattoo was hidden beneath his shirt sleeve. Cody Brock was a man who knew how to love, even if he forgot to say the words.

"You were promised to me when I was twelve years old," she whispered. "I might have gotten sidetracked along the way, forgotten to *believe*, but I believe now. And I love you.''

His sculpted lips curved into a slow, blinding smile. "So, what could be better than two people in love?"

This time it was Hallie who initiated a very public, very heated kiss. When she drew back, Cody's eyes were dilated to near black.

She stood on tiptoe and whispered in his ear, "How about the bad girl marrying the boy next door?"

"Ooo-rah!" Cody shouted. "She said yes!"

The crowd erupted with applause. Over the sound, Hallie heard the tinkling of bells, a mystical sound like wind chimes blowing gently on the wings of love.

She linked her hand with Cody's. "There's some people I want you to meet."

When she turned, only Maggie, J.D., Clarissa and Conor remained. Sabrina was nowhere in sight.

"Where did she go?"

"Who?" Cody asked.

Clarissa, Maggie and Hallie all smiled. On the floor at their feet was a twinkle of gold. Hallie bent down and picked up the three sparkling bracelets, handing one to each of her friends.

All three women slipped a bracelet on their arm. An eternal circle. The symbol of a wedding ring. Enduring love.

"Guys," Hallie said softly, addressing her two best friends and their respective husbands, "I'd like you to meet Cody Brock, my next door neighbor and the man I'm going to marry."

She rested her palm on his chest, then inched it up

to the back of his head as his lips met hers, sealing the promise in a time-honored way. When he lifted his head, the love in his eyes was bright enough to blind.

"*SemperFi,* Hallie." Always faithful.

The magic had worked, after all.

Clarissa had her millionaire, Maggie had her cowboy...and Hallie Fortune had eyes only for the bad boy next door.

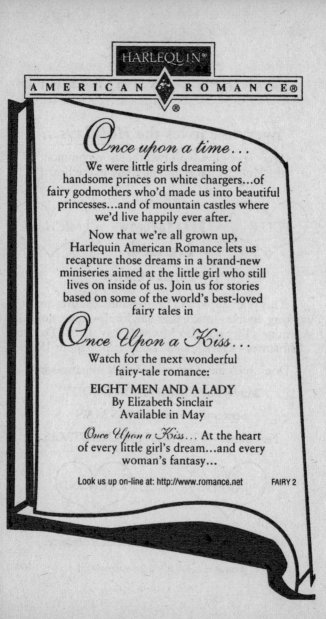

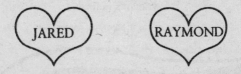

On the plus side, you've raised a
wonderful, strong-willed daughter.
On the minus side, she's using that
determination to find

A Match For
MOM

Three very different stories of mothers,
daughters and heroes...from three of your
all-time favorite authors:

GUILTY
by Anne Mather

A MAN FOR MOM
by Linda Randall Wisdom

THE FIX-IT MAN
by Vicki Lewis Thompson

Available this May wherever
Harlequin and Silhouette books are sold.

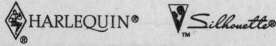

And the Winner Is...
You!

...when you pick up these great titles
from our new promotion at your
favorite retail outlet this June!

Diana Palmer
The Case of the Mesmerizing Boss

Betty Neels
The Convenient Wife

Annette Broadrick
Irresistible

Emma Darcy
A Wedding to Remember

Rachel Lee
Lost Warriors

Marie Ferrarella
Father Goose

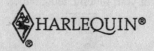